Way We Were

V S Mani

Michael Terence
Publishing

First published in paperback by
Michael Terence Publishing in 2022
www.mtp.agency

Copyright © 2022 V S Mani

V S Mani has asserted the right to be identified as the
author of this work in accordance with the
Copyright, Designs and Patents Act 1988

ISBN 9781800942905

No part of this publication may be reproduced, stored in
a retrieval system, or transmitted, in any form or by
any means, electronic, mechanical, photocopying,
recording or otherwise, without the prior
permission of the publishers

Cover image
V S Mani

Cover design
Copyright © Michael Terence Publishing

Contents

Preface

Authors appeal to the readers. It is fictional novel, not a romance, detective or crime thriller. Just everyday life in a select community in London in 50s and later. Please do not apply current day norms to people's behavior as it would lead to a big disappointment.

Synopsis

This novel "Way we were" deals with the way the people lived in the 50s to 70s. This is not a love or a detective story. It catalogues, the experiences, where the hero, "James", and his adopted parents, lived with the group of families who conformed to the thinking and behaviour of the swinging 60s. Apart from youngsters, many parents also mis-behaved to match the permissive society. James specialised in the skill of stock market trading. He met the heroine, Rose, a descendent of the Royal family, married her, and James with the help of Amma, Rose's mother, helped all the adults and youngsters in the group to a great extent. His tolerant and helpful attitude for adopted and LGBT children to remain independent and protected them from verbal abuses of the society. There is no real end to the story as it, like life, rambles on. Mercifully the author terminates the novel with a nice epilogue.

1
Prologue

A sultry night and the whole house seemed gripped in expectation of the baby's arrival. Tara, her husband Rajesh and Krishna waited on tenterhooks in the next room. Nearly an hour had passed since the senior nurse had taken the mother to the maternity ward with a Paediatrician. Tara's sister-in-law, Shantha, came to update them and told her husband Krishna that it would be a natural birth, not a caesarean, which brought a lot of relief to the family. 30 minutes later, a nurse announced the news they had all waited to hear, the safe delivery of a baby boy. He weighed 6lb 8 oz, measured 17 inches, had long fingers and toes and a very fair complexion.

Krishna, Shantha, Tara, and Ramesh returned home. Both the grandparents were there and delighted to hear the news. Krishna's parents named the baby Rama, as the boy was born on one of the most auspicious days in the Hindu religious calendar, Sri Rama Navami, the Lord Vishnu's avatar as a man.

***

Twelve years earlier

Krishna's dad arranged an Iyengar family marriage alliance for Krishna, who married Shantha from a profoundly religious but low-income family. Krishna invited all his friends, including Rajesh and his parents. They had lived in the same neighborhood for decades.

Nearly five years went by, but Shantha did not conceive. The community thought she was barren and asked Krishna to marry again. Rajesh, a medical doctor, arranged without Krishna's parents knowing, for Shantha to see a fertility clinic specialist. The specialist certified that Shantha could conceive children. With great reluctance, Krishna underwent a similar assessment and was found to be impotent. They considered adopting a child. However, Krishna's parents could not accept the fact of their son's impotence.

They all felt it was better to get a baby locally from Madras. In Madras, Krishna discovered there was a massive queue for adopting babies. The adoption agency said a wait for five to six years would be their best estimate. Krishna contacted agencies in other cities, but the period of waiting was longer. Getting an adoption certificate in Madras was costly. Tara agreed to fund the expenses if Shantha could find a needy family willing to give up their newborn baby for adoption.

Krishna registered with an adoption agency, and they said for IRS 80,000, they could have a baby to be born in 2 months. The mother did not even get 20% of the agency fees. When Krishna told Tara about the excessive charges, she spoke to the agent, who assured her that all certificates would be ready within a few days of the baby's delivery. The agency should receive the money after the baby's birth and the transfer of adoption certificates. Tara spoke to the family lawyer to clarify and make all things legal. The lawyer contacted the agency, and all arrangements were put in place. Tara transferred the money from her account to the lawyer, who confirmed receipt by the agency's lawyer. The lawyers ensured the agency received money and Shantha and Krishna received the adoption certificates. The mother did not want to see the baby as this was the second adoption procedure she had gone through.

Tara, an Iyengar girl, wanted to marry her childhood sweetheart, Rajesh, of an Iyer family, against her parent's wishes. It was frowned upon in those days, for such a mixed marriage. Her father threatened to disown her forever, but her mother could not bear to hear those harsh words. However, her father was very stubborn and was just about to push her out of the house, when her mother uncharacteristically shouted at the top of her voice that she would commit suicide if he did evict their daughter. Krishna proved no help to Tara, as he always sided with his dad against his mother's wishes, which annoyed her. Krishna's hatred of Rajesh grew from that day onwards, and they never spoke to each other.

Rajesh was a brilliant Oncology doctor. He went to the UK, where he soon became a consultant and had an excellent private practice in Harley Street as well as working in two hospitals in central London. Tara was brilliant academically and acquired a lecturing job at University College London (UCL). She had done a Master's in Mathematics and soon rose to become a Professor. They emigrated to the UK within a year of their marriage. They had a daughter after three years and another daughter two years later. Tara frequently spoke to her mother, but her dad and brother never communicated. Finally, Rajesh got his parents to join them, becoming UK citizens. Tara's dad, on the other hand, refused to set foot in the UK.

Krishna, at the age of almost 26, was incapable of making any decision without his dad's approval. He was not a good student, failed matriculation three times, discontinued further studies and only achieved a modest income working as an accounts clerk in a local government office. He shunned making new friends, his old friends ignored him and he was a loner, feeling pretty depressed and miserable with life. He was not religious and rarely recited the famous Vishnu Sahasranamam, the lifeline for the Iyengars. Krishna's dad was very disappointed but selected Shantha for her religious faiths and practices, having noticed her while visiting the temples. Her poor background did not worry his dad as he was only in the modest income group.

Shantha had a BA in Arts. She was good at singing, drawing and adept at tutoring children and adults on religious topics. She was good-looking and highly modest and never uttered a harsh word. Her standing in the community skyrocketed after her marriage. All the old friends of Rajesh and his dad started talking to them, which pleased both father and son. Despite all her endearing qualities, she could not talk about Tara and Rajesh. Shantha studied in the same class as Tara and admired her looks and good behavior. The school and the community expected Tara to marry Rajesh, it had been an open secret, so Krishna's dad's behavior and anger mystified everyone.

After Shantha's marriage, when her parents visited them, Shantha talked to her mother-in-law and mentioned Tara. Like lightning, Krishna's dad started a barrage of accusations and threatened her with expulsion from the house if she uttered Tara and Rajesh's names ever again. His wife got so annoyed, she shouted back at him, and he started beating her for the first time. Krishna could not tolerate this physical violence and pushed his dad away with such strength, the older man stumbled and fell backwards, hitting his head on the concrete floor and losing consciousness. They had to call an ambulance but he recovered quickly. They did all tests, scans, blood tests, etc and none of the results gave any cause for concern at the hospital. However, due to his high blood pressure and sweet tooth, his sugar levels shot up. He had swollen legs for a while but no one took any notice, more from ignorance than neglect, but within three days he was dead from kidney failure.

Tara wanted to come and pay respects to her dad, but Krishna refused to agree to Rajesh coming for the funeral. Finally, due to pressure from his mum and Shantha, he relented and agreed to a day's visit. He also wanted both to stay in a hotel and not with them in the house. Krishna's mum said that the house was still in her name, and she would decide who stayed in her place and for how long. She told Krishna to stay in the hotel if he disagreed, but her daughter and husband would only stay with her. Shantha pleaded with Krishna, and he softened his stance. He apologized profusely for being silly and promised to behave like a true brother and now the family's head. Shantha did not convey these verbal exchanges to Tara. Krishna's dad always wanted a simple funeral, for one day only, not for 13 days. He never wanted his little money swindled away by the religious people.

Tara, Rajesh, and his parents came and stayed in Krishna's place the next day. When Tara's mum saw her pregnant daughter, she was in tears, hugging her and crying. Everyone was emotional, even Krishna.

"Mum, I am sorry about dad's loss," said Tara, "our condolences to all. I am due to deliver the baby in four months and I would like you to come with us to the UK. We want both the grandmothers to be present to welcome the baby. We have only come for a week and we'd like to set everything in motion. I hope you have your Indian passport handy for me to look at later today?"

"Tara, let me get my breath back and enjoy the good news of the baby," replied her mum. "Regarding dad, I am sad in one way but relieved that the last 40 years of torture I suffered because of his stubbornness, hypocritical religious beliefs and forcing all of us to do what he wanted is over, and to me, it is a great relief. I want to go with you to the UK and it could be a long-haul visit. Unless Krishna changes his attitude and thinks and behaves respectfully, I will spend the rest of the days with you, Tara."

Krishna then surprised them all by standing up and addressing them.

"I wish to apologize to all of you. Firstly, to my mum for ruining her daily life playing second fiddle to my dad. To my sister, Tara, whose marriage happiness I spoiled by taking my dad's intransigence stance." Then he turned to Rajesh, the emotion clear in his voice, "To my school buddy of so many years whose marriage to Tara, I objected to, despite knowing they were high school sweethearts."

He paused to take in their astonished looks, before continuing,

"I did not allow Shantha to talk about Tara due to my dad's decree, as I never had an opinion of my own since my childhood days. I never made any decision, and I always followed whatever my dad dictated. I also apologize to Rajesh's parents for my bad behavior. I have decided to change from now on; Tara, seeing you brought my senses back. Mum, please go with Tara and enjoy the baby's birth, but please return to stay with us. Shantha can also go with you all if she wishes. Her parents can stay at our house from now on."

"Krishna," said Rajesh, beaming at his friend. "I am amazed at the total transformation in such a short time. Shantha has to apply for a passport, and we would like you to accompany her. Our stay could be extended to two weeks, if necessary, to sort out various formalities."

"So many good things have happened since your arrival, Tara," said her mum. "Let the ceremonies be over tomorrow, then we can plan. I have a few important things to discuss later tomorrow. After that, it is time to have dinner and go to sleep as tomorrow we have an early start at 5 am."

Tara was so happy to sleep in her room with Rajesh, and she had an hour bonding session with her friend Shantha before going to bed. Rajesh enjoyed a similar session with Krishna before he went to bed. The following day all the solemn ceremonies were over by midday. Tara paid for the priests and all other expenses. She also gave Krishna five lacs of rupees to cover all the costs incurred. She knew his income was meagre and Shantha was not allowed to work by her dad.

After lunch and a short siesta, Tara arranged for the local travel agent to come, who got the various details from Shantha and Krishna and filled in their passport applications. The agent said she would come in two weeks to get the applications filled in for visas for going to the UK. Tara gave her mum's passport to obtain a permit to visit the UK. The agent told her that it would take three weeks to get a British visa. Tara decided that the three of them should travel together to London, and she paid the agent the fares for the three. After an early dinner, they sat in the lounge for discussions.

Tara's mum began, "I want to sort out two critical issues following your dad's demise: his Will and my decisions following that. Your dad had very little free cash, and he did not have much life cover. The insurance company will pay IRs 15,000 to our joint account in a month. The house is an ancestral property, and he did not make much money. It passes to me and then to you and Krishna. We should see the lawyer tomorrow and clarify, to reassure me before you both leave."

As her mum wished, Tara met with the lawyer and found out that she and Krishna had to pay the estimated estate duty of

40% on her mum's death, which would amount to IRS 8 lacs. As Krishna would not share, she agreed to pay the amount appropriately. They all talked for an hour and felt it was the best discussion they had, but this would never have happened if her dad had not passed away.

The next few days continued happily and Tara, Rajesh, and his parents returned to London. They were in regular telephone contact keeping abreast of passports and visa situations. These were ready in six weeks, and the four, including the child Rama, arrived in the UK on a Saturday, seven weeks later. Everything was new to them and they admired the cleanliness, lack of the sound of horns, and traffic sticking to lanes and giving signals before changing lanes. They enjoyed Tara and Rajesh's spacious house and the tv programs so different from those of Madras.

Tara was growing bigger by the day. Rajesh had arranged all the facilities for the safe delivery of the baby in the hospital. The baby arrived without any delay and it was an expected delivery. Rajesh's parents named her Priya. She was fair, 7lb 9 oz, 17 in long, lovely dimples, possibly with curly hair when she grows up, they all thought. After four weeks, Tara's brother returned to Madras and his mum and wife followed six weeks later.

After three years, she gave birth to another pretty girl, Asha, a lot fairer, 8lb 8oz, 16 in long. Tara's mother came for six months and doted on the two babies. The sisters grew up very affectionate, and Priya was always protective of Asha. Finally, Tara and Rajesh decided to have no more children. They started to focus on the two and brought them up nicely.

The years rolled on and Tara's family visited them for a few months every two years.

2
A wave of despair

On one of the festive days, four thugs barged into Krisha's house and demanded money. As people were rejoicing in the streets, no outsiders observed the intruders in the commotion. Fortunately, Rama was asleep upstairs. Each thug brandished a sharp 9-inch knife. Instead of handing over any cash they had, Krishna and Shantha's dad resisted. Shantha and her mum tried to stop their husbands from fighting, but the thugs misunderstood and each thug knifed the four of them and fled with IRS 15000. No one noticed anything for several hours till a neighbor heard Rama crying and saw the four bleeding dead bodies. The police and social services came. The police cordoned off the house and social services took care of Rama. A police officer got Tara's address and told her the grim news. The social services refused to talk to her as they could not confirm Tara's relationship with the baby.

Tara and her family came to Madras and performed the last rites for the four. The lawyers helped Tara sort out the low insurance payments due for Krishna and Shantha's dad, which amounted to IRS 12000 only, and the house would have gone to Rama and Tara. Still, the social services would not accept the money under his name and put in a fixed deposit under his name for future allocations. However, they would guarantee to pay the boy with all interest gained. They said the interest rate in the post office account was 12% per annum.

Tara and her family were very disappointed, and the agency

said they understood their anger at the system. Tara felt that she lost her investment of IRS 80,000 within a year, with no recourse to finding the boy. They all returned to the UK, hoping the boy named Rama would rise from all the challenges he would have to face in his life. Tara visited Madras each year as she rented out her ancestral house through a reputable agent to an international company at a reasonable rent for five years. Each year she tried to locate the boy Rama to no avail. Finally, after five years, she gave up as a lost cause, and after two years, Rama faded from everyone's memory.

***

It is time to follow up on Rama's life.

The Social Services took him to their premises for care. A very wealthy British couple living in Calcutta was the first in line to adopt. They were impressed with Rama's growth and readily accepted. Rama was very fair, with no trace of darkness in color. However, they were sad to note the circumstances, and the adoption agency did not divulge the previous adopted parents' names. Instead, they wanted the child named James with their names, John and Mary Smith, as parents on the adoption certificate.

After paying the amount due, the couple with Rama returned to their palatial house in New Alipore. Their parents were no more, and neither of them had any siblings. Both the parents were over the moon as Rama's development was a lot faster than the other children of his age. John Smith was the MD of a large British company, and Mary was religious to the core. She appointed an Indian religious lady to teach James all slokas to recite with utmost devotion and without errors or missing words. He had a sweet musical voice. They admitted James to a prestigious English school. The company wanted John to manage the International Division in London. Within four years of the adoption, they were in London. The company mansion was in St. John's Wood, a six-bedroomed house with all mod cons built to American specifications. They employed a maid cum childminder for James.

The couple were delighted, thinking James' arrival had brought all the good luck with the job and increased income. Mary was very relaxed, and soon she gave birth to a boy, Robert, and a girl within four years, Susan.

James was ten years old when Robert was born. Life was bliss for the next five years. James was doing well in school and was interested in stocks and shares. John set up a small fund for James to play around with, and Mary handled the stock buying and selling as per James's instructions. She found that he doubled his investment of £1,000 in a few months. Robert found their mum devoting more time to James than to him, he became difficult to manage, and he started hating James. John advised Mary to forget stock trading and focus on Robert. Despite 100% focus on Robert, his truancy did not stop. It only escalated with more of his mum's attention. He was difficult to control in school and hard for teachers to handle. Robert did not get on with Susan, as she clung to James most of the time. Robert would not talk to James, and in the last few months, he became violent and started attacking James and Susan.

Despite having a specialist nurse for over a year, Robert did not change. He would not talk to his mum or dad. One evening when the children had gone to bed, the parents discussed the situation.

"Mary, I was told by my colleague to separate James from the other children and try six to nine months. He had to do this with his 3rd child, a daughter, and they found a lot of improvement in her violent behavior. Then they brought the other two back from their grandma, and all the three got on a bit better after that. So, I told him their grandparents were no more, and we did not have any siblings to send the children."

"I am not sure we have a relative or a close friend to send James and Susan to," replied Mary. "It is no point in sending them to a boarding school, even for a short period. It is better to keep Robert downstairs, including breakfast and dinner, and keep James and Susan upstairs, including breakfast and dinner. As Susan is attached to James, she will not miss me much and for that, we should be grateful to James."

"Let's follow your instinct," replied her husband, "and you could have an assistant to take care of the two. Maybe you could hire a cook and use the present maid, who knows the children, as your assistant and increase her salary?"

Mary agreed with the choice of the assistant and gave him a warm hug. John remarked that hugs were becoming very infrequent after three children and enjoyable when it happened. They found that their maid as the new assistant for upstairs was agreeable to James and Susan.

A few months rolled by, and Robert began to understand that he was not playing with his siblings after school anymore, but he could hear James and Susan running around upstairs and laughing. Robert told his mum he wanted to join them, so she allowed him to go upstairs. The three children played happily for a few hours. From that day onwards, all saw a marked change in Robert. He even wanted to sleep upstairs and share their beds sometimes. The school teachers also reported a significant difference in his behavior; he was no longer aggressive or depressed. Robert started listening to James and learned slokas to recite and pray to the various Gods. Both mum and dad were delighted, and they felt they were leading an everyday happy family life twelve years after James's arrival.

Slowly, Robert started respecting James and was affectionate towards Susan. The three were inseparable from that time onwards which was a relief to the parents and the staff. Mary began to help James with stock trading. Being older Robert and Susan started to understand money and James's skills. They were very excited when the stock value increased. Mary told them not to say anything to outsiders or friends about this. To make them understand James's skills more, she told James that he should show how £1,000 changes and explained. They were very excited and were checking the stock every few minutes. Mary felt their concentration had changed from studies to stock values. Realizing this, James said he would let them know when trading closed each day, and realistically, he usually checked the share value at the end of each Friday and sold before trading closed. They were a bit disappointed, but James kept them informed.

James also told them that he would reveal the results each day after they had completed their daily homework. Reluctantly, they agreed. Their results in the school also improved significantly and they received a lot of praise from the Head Teacher. James was always at the top of the class, and he merited 50% to 100% scholarships for each year. James was able to mould Robert and Susan more than his mum or dad, which delighted them.

We have to roll back several years to when John and Mary came to London. Mary admitted the children to an expensive public school. Mary met the Head Teacher, who recommended seeing Nancy. Mary and Nancy were very friendly from that time onwards. Nancy was an associate professor in the

Department of Chemistry, and her husband, Jeff, was a professor of Physics, and both were in Imperial College. They both studied in the same college, and the university love resulted in their marriage seven years ago. After nine years, they had Liz (Elizabeth) followed by Peter three years later, and Margaret three years after that. The six children, James, Robert and Susan, Liz, Peter, and Margaret, bonded closely. They all went to the same private school and did 'O' and 'A' levels.

Because of James's fair appearance, people took him to be Caucasian rather than Indian. In school, he made many friends among the British boys and girls. He was able to help students with exam revisions, and they and the teachers were very impressed with him. In Cambridge, he specialized in Finance and Management, and the Professor was astonished at his skill in stock market investment. He was encouraged by the head of the department to take ad hoc lectures in the evening for interested students, and to their surprise, not only students but outsiders attended. James was paid a notional amount for the lessons, which he donated to the student welfare fund.

When James was studying in 8th standard, children of Indian origin and British nationality joined his school. Tara and her family had known Nancy and her family, as their next-door neighbor in the posh area of St. Johns's Wood. Tara's girls were in a private school. Nancy recommended that the school her children were studying at had better 'O' and 'A' level results, so Tara changed her two girls to that school. After a few days, Tara met Mary in the new school, and the children got to know each other quite well. They also learned about James's skills and how he was doing very well in his studies. Slowly all came to James with their queries and he explained better than the teachers. Finally, all the teachers noticed his skills and allowed James to teach students to help with their homework after school.

One day, Mary spilt the news of James's skills on share market dealings, by a slip of the tongue. The teacher was most impressed and joined a few of his share dealing sessions and was astonished to find a genius in the school. However, due to Mary's persistent requests, she stopped talking about it on the proviso he would deal with her investment of £2,000 with no penalty for losing the investment. Mary said James should be trading with investors' money once he reached the age of 21. However, she found it a strain to do on his behalf. The Head Teacher agreed but saw how his shares were progressing. Because the Head Teacher saw James frequently, the students started to call him 'teacher's pet.' He disliked the term, but he could not control the whole school and only very few agreed to his appeal not to use the word.

Mums started noticing the girls were getting too close to the boys and could sense problems ahead if not nipped in the bud. The three mums discussed and agreed that James was more sensible for his age and asked if he would deal with the issue. He needed some time to mull over it and wanted the mums to be frank with him and explain clearly the issues involved. Is some association not recommended, or were they too young to commit themselves?

"Both Priya and Asha are interested in you," said Tara. "Of the two, Asha being good at Mathematics, is likely to spend more time with you and develop a closer relationship, giving rise to unnecessary issues between the sisters."

"My children are young enough to worry about now," added Nancy. "Whatever James decides, I will accept without reservation."

"I'm not sure about Robert due to his early years," said Mary. "Even though he has changed for the better, thanks to James's guidance. Susan is too young to worry about for now."

"I have a novel solution," said James. "And I'd like to have all the boys and girls present here before I explain."

The mothers agreed and asked all the children to join them.

"We three families are very close-knit," started James, "and we should behave as brothers and sisters. There should never be any other thoughts on relationships amongst us. We should all feel proud that we have such good brothers and sisters, and we should behave like true brothers shielding our sisters when they need our help."

They all agreed, and the mums were very pleased with the clever solution, feeling confident for their daughters' future. All the boys and girls were also happy with the brothers and sisters they had picked up. After the pep talk by James, the three families spent weekends and holidays together, which improved the bonding amongst the families and the children.

Slowly the other families began to know about James's skill in share dealings. Finally, Mary told them to wait until he reached 21, and they agreed. Asha was most interested in trading and followed his weekly results. She followed the strategy used by James meticulously. She wrote all the steps, and after trading hours, she still read the comments and forecasts for the next day. James realized Asha was very conscientious and disciplined. None of her focus affected her studies as she scored top marks like James in school and college.

Five years later, Priya, at 21 was studying medicine at UCL and in her final year. She wanted to be a Paediatrician. Asha, at 18 was a 2nd-year student at Cambridge studying Computer Science. Priya enjoyed dealing with the patients and making copious notes for records. She enjoyed talking to the midwives, pregnant mothers waiting for the delivery, and mothers who had delivered their babies. Sadly, she also spoke to mothers who lost their babies. All these cast a lasting impression on her. She saw patients and gave medication after consulting with the doctor in charge. Her confidence grew day by day, and she enjoyed every minute of the hospital experience.

Asha was outstanding in mathematics and took to computer courses like a duck to water, like her mother. She was good at writing programs and troubleshooting when required. In addition, she specialized in the testing and implementation of software.

Jeff and Nancy's close friends were Dennis and Peggy. Dennis was the owner of a manufacturing company located near Uxbridge underground station. Peggy was a chartered accountant for that company but primarily worked from home. Their two sons, Russel and Trevor, worked in their dad's company as section heads for Personnel and Finance, respectively. Russel had done a Masters's in Management and Finance, and Trevor was a Certified Accountant. They had frequent contact with the other boys and girls, and Dennis was keen to get James to work for him.

One evening, all the boys and girls were in Dennis's house for dinner with their parents. After dinner, they gathered in the living room for a discussion.

"I've heard many good things about you, James," said Dennis. "You're a wise investor. I would like you to work for my company and head the new investment section. You name your salary for me to consider and please call me Dennis from now on."

"Dear Dennis," replied James, "I am flattered to receive this fantastic offer of such a lucrative job. However, I'm afraid I've decided not to accept it."

"James, are you sure you want to refuse such an offer?" said John, taken aback by his son's decision.

"Do you want more time to think about it?" asked Mary, gently.

"Mum, Dad, I have a clear idea of what I want to do in the future. Also, I know what I *do not* want to do. I have two options and both involve working from home. Firstly, I want to have my own company using private investors' money to trade in the stock markets, UK - FTSE, USA - Dow and NASDAQ, India and the Far East. Trading in these markets would mean I would have to work from 7 am to 10 pm and read up about stocks in these markets.

"Secondly, that I work for Mr Dennis's and his contact's private savings, but again working from home. I want a good quality of life without the stress of commuting, office politics and related corporate pressures. Dennis, I must also caution you that the yearly return may not be more than 10%. Rarely would it reach 20%."

"I'm impressed with your second option," smiled Dennis. "Please manage my private fund of 1 million in the first year, and if successful, I will invest £5 million. My friends would invest about £2 million. I will review it every six months. My company lawyers will send you the papers to operate as a subsidiary of my company but with an independent identity as the sole controller. You will report to me directly. Your return of even 10% yearly is good enough for me and my contacts."

"I have prepared a document for trading with all the conditions for investors," said James, also with a smile. "They will receive a copy before they invest with me. Dennis, also, I need a monthly payment of £2,500. I hope you agree to this? I would also need to modify my room to install the new IBM golf-ball typewriter equipment. I prefer to operate as totally independent of the parent company to take care of my tax, pension, NI, etc. Therefore, I do not need a car from the company as I would pay for those expenses.

"I will have this document printed out for new investors. At the moment the investors have to contact me. Later, I will designate a person and I will only see the investment amount."

"James, I agree to all your terms," said Dennis. "But please move to my house, and you will have a small self-contained flat. You will operate from a room adjacent to my office, with all the up-to-date facilities. You can plan to move from next month, and there will be no rental charge. I also have an annexe building with a large self-contained flat, so you can choose either of those accommodations.

"I'd prefer to stay in the annexe building," replied James, "and I'd like an Indian cook to prepare spicy foods. I would work in the main office. I also choose to have a modern IBM typewriter facility in the annexe building."

"I'm surprised you didn't choose to stay with us in the main complex and share our lives, James."

"I feel you should be able to discuss family matters confidently without an outsider present. There are times you may have strong disagreements, quarrels, etc., and my presence would only dampen the discussions. Also, you would all rather I stayed in the annexe, and why I shall tell you later."

"I agree to charge £500 monthly for the annexe accommodation," said Dennis. "All the paperwork will be ready to check and sign before starting the new operation in a week.

Is there anything else anyone would like to add?"

"I have something personal to tell you all which may come as a bit of a shock," replied James. "I think it's better coming from me, so you get it from the horse's mouth! My first-time adopted parents in Calcutta met with untimely deaths four years after my adoption. My parents, John and Mary, re-adopted me in Calcutta about 25 years ago. The adoption agencies did not show the details of my first adoption, but I managed to get the facts from the officer-in-charge, as I promised to double his investment within nine months, which I did, and that was two years ago. I still take care of his investment. I learned that my biological mother died ten years ago of vaginal cancer. There were no relations found of her nor any siblings.

"My life as the son of my mum and dad, you all know very well. The news might come as a surprise or shock to Robert and Susan. My depth of feelings for both of them will not change; I would willingly play the third fiddle in the family hierarchy. I only found out about all of this about two years ago. Mum and dad already know everything. I asked them for their approval to reveal all this, yesterday evening. They agreed that it was better coming from me.

"I was also planning to move out of the house and get my own apartment for trading. So, the timing was right to make this announcement. I did not know about Dennis's offer of a job then, but somehow it blended nicely with my revelations. You should all know that my lineage is not something I say with pride. My present adopted mum and dad have given me the respectability to move with you as part of your group. A few years ago, my appeal to all of you to treat everyone as brothers or sisters, no longer applies in my case due to my questionable lineage. I will take no offence if you all choose to ignore me. However, my fond feelings for you all will never diminish, and

I will be there for you, whenever you need me."

"James, you brightened our lives from the day we adopted you," said Mary. "All the good things that happened, John's job, he was asked to move to London, the large house in this salubrious area, etc., happened so quickly and we would never focus on your lineage. After adoption, a wife can become pregnant, and we were pleased to have Robert and then Susan. You are our eldest son, and your moving out will not change anything."

"Dear James," said Tara, suddenly. "You were first adopted by my brother Krishna and his wife, Shantha. Your birth mother used to sell babies for adoption, and you were her second child. She did not want to see or cuddle you despite requests by the nurses. She also did not reveal the name of the father. Rajesh and I paid IRS 80,000 to the adoption society, and you were born on the birthday of Lord Rama. We are Iyengars, and my father named you Rama. When you were four years old, the tragedy struck."

She narrated all the events till they settled in the UK.

"We tried to locate you, but the adoption society would not reveal any details, and in the end, we were forced to give up."

"I am so happy to know about my first adoption and the first four years of my life. Aunty, I am delighted to meet you and be in your company!" smiled James.

"How strange we have known each other for some time, Tara but never knew you had the background information about Rama before we adopted. We changed his name to James at the time of adoption."

"I am shocked by James's revelations," said Robert. "But for me, it is all water under the bridge. I had a difficult childhood, and James sorted out those issues for me, for good. So, I am indebted to my elder brother for life. His lineage is neither here nor there."

"And I owe you so much James, for helping me do better in my exams all these years," said Susan, tearfully. "Like Robert, I am indebted to you and your lineage makes no difference to me."

"This has been an evening of astonishing revelations," smiled Nancy, "and I understand there will be many more to follow. The boys and girls are all over 18 now and able to decide on their future. James' lineage would not alter our respect and regard for him as he is the gem of our families."

Robert did not want to go to Uni, and he had befriended Debbie from the time of their 'O' levels. Her parents were impressed with him and his family. Debbie's dad, Keith, had a large farm in South Africa, and he wanted Robert to join his business there, so Robert planned to leave with Debbie to work and live in South Africa, within a month. Keith also owned a large farm in Zimbabwe that his eldest son, Arthur, managed. He was in love with Liz, who specialized in Personnel Management in Oxford. Liz was going to Zimbabwe in a month to help him. Susan did a Master's in Business Management; she was in love with Peter, who did not want to go to the university. However, his good looks and pleasant personality helped him to secure an excellent job in Barclays Bank in the Accounts department. Russel studied Economics and International Relations, and he was in love with Priya. Trevor did not want to go to university, but he was so attractive, Asha fell for him. Russel wanted to marry Priya and Trevor wanted to marry Asha. Dennis and Peggy were happy with the wedding of their boys and with Priya and Asha working for the company.

Mary and Nancy felt that only James and Margaret were still unattached in their group of boys and girls.

25

3
No starry, starry nights

James started work in his new office in the annexe building and found all the facilities better than imagined. He was requested to have lunch or tea with the family, but he refused. Finally, they realized that he was very focused on his job. James never wasted a moment on idle gossip or small talk. Peggy felt that the more she moved with James, the more she became aware of his strengths and good nature. Both Peggy and Dennis admired how a child with no lineage could be a model son to all. After a few weeks, Dennis invited everyone to dinner, as all the boys and girls were in London at the same time. That evening, they all gathered for pre-dinner drinks.

"Rajesh and I are glad that our two girls will still be living in this area after their marriages to Dennis and Peggy's boys," said Tara.

"John and I discussed that, too, Tara," said Mary. "Robert and Susan, after their weddings to Keith and Joanne's boy and girl, will be leaving the UK to live abroad. At least we are glad James will be nearby in Dennis's annexe building, next door to us. Still, the house will seem very empty soon."

"Jeff and I know," said Nancy, "that when Liz marries Keith and Jo's son, Arthur, she will be living abroad. But at least Peter will be with us and Margaret's still unattached, so far."

"If I might be audacious and suggest something to Keith and Jo?" said James. "With the very threatening conditions existing for British and other foreign nationals owning lands and farms in Southern Africa, why not get rid of the farms and buy similar properties here in the UK? It would be a lot safer and you will all enjoy a much better quality of life here."

"It's a brilliant suggestion, James, given the unrest in both South Africa and Rhodesia. Thank you for putting it forward," said Dennis.

"James, I'm glad you raised this question too," agreed Keith. "Jo and I have been worried about living there and we are nearly in the finishing stages of the sale. In a month, we should sell both. So, Mary, your wish will come true, all your family will be living in the UK. We hope to buy farms nearer here. James is like a son to all of us, focussing on each family's best interests."

"I'm glad that our three families, with boys and girls studying in the same school have ended up here, even after their weddings," said Dennis.

"We're expecting Clare, a school friend of Margaret's to join us for dinner," said James. "This is at Margaret's and my invitation. Sorry to spring this surprise on you, Dennis and Peggy."

Clare soon arrived and Dennis and Peggy gave her a warm welcome. After all the introductions and welcomes were over, she accepted a glass of punch and sat down next to Margaret, who then addressed all of them.

"I have asked my brother, James, to speak on my behalf. He has always been a rock to me all these years."

Everyone looked at James, wondering what was to follow.

"The news I will share with you needs understanding and compassion," he said, "for all the parties involved. As they say, this is how the cookie crumbles. Margaret and Clare have been in a lesbian relationship for some years. We have to understand and give them all the support they need. Anything less and we risk driving them out to be lost forever from our families. They are too precious for us to lose. We need all the resolve to face this situation, which might be unusual for us but is quite common in the wider world. I will always remain a supportive brother to both of them from now on."

Margaret cleared her throat, nervously. "I asked James to break the news to all of you in my presence so that you hear it directly. Clare is part of my life, and we have no regrets."

"You have never met me until now," said Clare. "But I hope we will both be part of the fabric of your families from now on. We both are very good artists. James had sold a few paintings on our behalf and with his help, we started a limited company. Margaret and I own the company and James feels we could both be mega earners from now on. He will restructure the company soon and invest £25,000 with a 5% shareholding. James sold two of our paintings for £6,000 and we were over the moon. He seems to have excellent contacts and could sell the pictures at attractive prices. He wants to ask his mum to be the Company Accountant and manage the company's day-to-day running at a modest salary with NI and pension benefits."

"I wish both of you, Margaret, and Clare the best of British luck in your relationship," said Dennis warmly, "and I'd like to invest £25,000 for a 5% share like James."

Soon, Keith, Tara and Mary chipped in for a 5% share each and within minutes, the new company had funds from investors of £125,000.

"Well," said Dennis, "I have to marvel at the strategy of James in breaking the delicate news about Margaret and Clare, then redirecting our views to the new company formation and very tempting shareholding."

"It is nice to earn an income at this late stage in my life," agreed Mary, "and yes, we do indeed have to marvel at James's planning."

"As a parent," said Nancy, "I took the initial news with a lot of trepidation and concern, but James packaged the information, so I forgot about the news and was more interested in the new company and its performance."

Margaret and Clare came and hugged James.

"Dennis," he said, as he left their embrace, "even though I stay in the annexe, I work in the main office. So, I'd like to ask you two favors. Firstly, I'd like to stay at my house and come to the main office for work. Your house is only a five-minute walk away. Secondly, I'd like Margaret and Clare to occupy the annexe and use the office for their business. In that way, I would have a good handle on their business. In addition, their company would pay the rent. I hope these would be agreeable to all the parties?"

"James, your mind is always thinking of better plans for all of us," replied Dennis. "They can occupy as of tomorrow. You have solved their accommodation problem at a stroke, which is very praiseworthy."

"Clare and I thank you, James, for our accommodation to live together from tomorrow and for the office to work," smiled Margaret.

"My mum need not come to the office every day, as she can do her job from home," added James, "and then she could come to the office when it is essential."

The maid announced that dinner was ready. After dinner and coffee, they all left for their homes. Nancy wanted a short meeting for an hour or so with just Margaret, Clare, Mary and James; none of the others was to crash in. When the five were in Nancy's house, the maid closed the lounge door for greater privacy.

"As a mother," started Nancy immediately, "my mind is racing with all scenarios of objections, rude and disparaging remarks from friends and relatives, and my mind is not at peace."

"Aunty, your mind will never be at peace for any length of time," responded James. "Peace of mind for a short duration is possible till you hear an unpleasant comment. No one needs to know about them immediately, and their working together for their new company would keep others quiet. They should control their excitement and never kiss or hold hands in public. They should always question what is important to them, their long-term relationship or making the wide world know about them? My advice is to play it low key as the relationship is more important. All the close families here would be supportive, and aunty, your mental peace would never be troubled."

"I agree with you, James," said Clare, "but there might be occasions when we might want to go shopping or even to a cafe."

"You both are around 21 years of age," he said. "Until you both reach 30, society will not question the mother about your marriage. Your business venture would shield you both and your mother from awkward questions. Also, you both should take rudimentary precautions. Have escorts like Liz or me to avoid focusing on you as a couple. You both have lovely privacy in the ample annexe accommodation. If you both walk outside holding hands or kissing, then aunty, you can forget about mental peace from that day onwards.

"You both would have to inform your GP about this relationship, as the NHS would view you differently. Confidentiality from the GP practice is crucial, and the GP should advise the staff accordingly. Clare should register with the same GP as Margaret. Sometimes GPs flag up by denoting LGBT (Lesbian, Gay, Bi-sexual, and Transgender). You both should request the GPs not to flag up in the notes with LGBT lest other receptionists notice that and start gossiping."

"James, how come you know so much about this?" asked Mary, surprised.

"Mum, in the college, two boys were Gay, and they found I was the only one sympathetic to them. So, they talked freely and told me about informing the GPs. The hatred of the general public for Gays is very significant. Compared to that, the attitude towards lesbians is more tolerant."

"Did they say anything else?" asked Margaret.

"Yes, more about the Gays," replied James. "However, one could extend some parts to the lesbians. They implied that there would be frequent threats once they know you two are lesbians; many older women might tend to break your relationship so that for an older woman to associate with the younger woman. The threat is for both of you. So, be sure of your relationship and maintain a solid, unbreakable bond."

"As our big brother, James, please guide us from time to time on the various pitfalls we may have to overcome lest we unnecessarily split due to bad judgment," said Clare. "We both have to bat for a very long inning, in cricket parlance. You very shrewdly put us in the annexe. What prompted you to decide on that?"

"I heard about your background in Bernado's and what a struggle you had having lost your parents at the tender age of 5 years. You were a good student, and this skill made them give special treatment and consideration to you. As a result, you got the scholarship to study in this private school and develop a friendship with Margaret."

"As a mother," said Nancy, "I did not guess their relationship even though Clare came to my house and attended the family events. James, you could think and act to understand them without revealing them to any one of us."

"I guessed about six years ago and spoke to both. They initially felt guilty and did not want to talk to me. I reassured them about total confidentiality, and they only started confiding in me. I had made some money in trading. I contacted Bernado's, funded £1,000 and expressed my interest in the welfare of Clare. I slowly built up a confidential relationship with the Head of Bernado's and had further information about her background. In a way, I was comparing my early life with her. I consider myself extremely lucky to have parents like John and Mary, who are very affluent. In contrast, Clare had undergone many struggles, ended up without adopted parents, but came out smelling of roses! I salute her and I'll make sure she does not experience any more bad periods, financially, socially, or emotionally."

Clare walked over to James and showered him with kisses on his cheeks! Mary, Margaret and Nancy followed with hugs and kisses too. After that, Mary and James went home and Clare stayed with Margaret but alone in the guest room.

The following day, Margaret and Clare moved into the annexe flat. Each occupied a separate bedroom as James advised not to give any clues to the cleaners the next day about being together. James had two rooms modified to suit the two painters. All modern materials, sets and kits, drawing sets, brushes, pigments, varnishes, glues, safety and cleaning, stocked for convenient access. He also asked the gardener to plant many flowers and lay them out for a pleasant walk by the two artists. Mary, Nancy and Peggy supervised the work. James had advised avoiding close contact between the two of them while in the garden and not attracting any staff's attention.

For several weeks they focussed on painting natural scenes and typical garden scenery. Then Margaret wanted to branch out, painting portraits and sometimes models. Clare wanted to stick to the reproduction of the painting of Great Masters. They had to practise the new type of paintings for a few weeks, as both knew. James wanted to talk to them with his mum for a few hours, and he asked one of the maids in the house not to allow anyone to the annexe. Clare made a nice cup of filter coffee for all.

"One of my investors has recommended a venture capitalist firm for marketing the paintings from both of you," announced James. "It is their way of investing in your company. They have good contacts with companies in the UK, USA, Europe, Japan, Oz and Sotheby's. They agreed to take care of the marketing and negotiating the selling prices, but they would deduct 20% as their commission based on the gross price. They would also recommend clients who have a specific requirement for reproduction paintings and portraits, and sometimes they may send models for pictures. A few times, the need may be for a nude painting, illustration, art, etc. Many times, this would be on a canvas. My suggestion to both of you is that typically reproduction paintings will command a higher price than portraits. Each one sticking to one type of painting only, there will be a significant disparity in incomes; both of you should do both types of paintings and alternate to even out payments."

"James," replied Clare, "you have made it easier for us not to worry about the clients. We focus only on the paintings. I can see the benefit of alternating to even out the earnings for both."

"I would ensure there is a record of profit per order and credit whoever completed the order and every six months do income apportioning to be fair to both of you," said Mary. "It is a very tricky point, James. Taking precautions from the beginning would avoid conflicts between the two on money aspects."

"Being a Venture Capitalist," Margaret chipped in, "did they agree to pay our company some minimum monthly amount to cover salaries for the two of us?"

"Yes," replied James. "They agreed to pay each of you £2,000 per month for a year and review. They will terminate their contract if the income is below their investment in the year. No repayment of any money advanced was required."

"It seems a win-win situation for both of them," smiled Mary. "James, I think you should also take a monthly salary."

"I will wait for you both to make a hefty profit," he said, "and invest with me. 10% commission on that should be enough for me. They are sending the contract for the three of you to sign tomorrow. After that, the two of you have to attend various exhibitions and auctions to promote your images and potential sales."

"We both agree," said Margaret. "And James should earn £2,000 per month like ours and Margaret £500 per month."

"James, you seem to have made our jobs more manageable,"

said Clare, "and we thank you. However, it is time to close this meeting and relax as tomorrow could be an eventful day."

The next day, at 10 am, the two owners Ralph and Stanley arrived and brought the contracts for the three to sign. James was just an observer. They explained their intended visits to a museum displaying their paintings to Margaret and Clare. They also left four Grand Masters for reproduction and four for portraits, and the models would be visiting the studio after agreeing to the dates and times convenient to Margaret.

A very stunning and slim-looking lady arrived to see James and introduced herself as Rose Butler.

"Please, call me James," he said. "How may I help you? Please give me your details too."

"James, I heard so much about you from the Venture Capitalist, Ralph," she said. "My mum and dad were in poor health, so I cared for our property and business. My elder brother is married and devotes more time to drinks, smoking and gambling; my younger brother is doing A levels and is an average student. I have done a Masters in Economics and Finance at London Business School.

Ralph's company is running our company and charges 20% commission. They have managed very well in the last two years, and we are delighted. Now I want to invest a modest £10,000 and review your returns."

"I could get returns of only 6% in a year," replied James, "which you might get from other investors. You might even do better with the others."

"I am happy with whatever returns you could get."

"I am glad about investing with me, and please read my

contract for trading. I would get a typed contract for both of us to sign today or tomorrow, and a copy to sign would be ready in 30 minutes. Please give the company's names, address details and your name, Rose, to the secretary."

She complied immediately.

"I'll wait and see the contract here and sign it."

James asked the maid to offer coffee or tea and biscuits to Rose, which she accepted, and by the time she finished, the secretary brought a few copies of the contract. Rose read the two-page agreement drafted in simple terms. She was delighted and signed two copies for James's company and two for her company.

At that moment, Margaret and Clare walked into James's office. James introduced both of them and they were stunned by her looks. They clarified a few doubts about their contracts and were about to leave when Rose offered to walk with them to their office. She eventually spent an hour with them, and they told her a lot about James. They noticed Rose was happy hearing the details of James and showed an interest in him. She left after a while and asked her chauffeur to pick her up.

Mary came to know about Rose from James, as an investor recommended by Ralph, the venture capitalist. He talked about the business side, but Margaret and Clare felt Rose was romantically attracted to him, something he refused to accept. Mary prayed that James would find a suitable girl to marry and secretly talked to John.

After telephoning, Rose came to see John, bringing many documents to open a joint account with BSL, as James suggested. The process took about three hours. She had lunch with Margaret and Clare, while James had lunch with his mum.

After lunch BSL confirmed the various details for operating the account, usually only sent by post, which meant a delay of at least three working days. Rose asked if she could be an assistant and learn to trade stocks. James smiled and said he could train her but would pay no salary.

"Thank you, Shylock," she said, smiling back.

"15, love to you, Rose," he quipped.

Unexpectedly, she tried to hug James and kiss him but he managed to free himself and escape her strong embrace before she landed the kiss.

"This sort of behavior in the office is a sackable offence," he said with mock severity. "Common sense should prevail. Any repetition and you will no longer be required to come to this office for training."

Smilingly, she apologized and promised it would not happen again, but she enjoyed every second of teasing him.

"I start work at 7 am to deal with UK stocks, noon to 10 pm on the USA stocks and later for Fast Eastern stocks," he said, getting down to business.

"Do you think I should stay here with you not miss any part of the training?"

"Trading is a grave matter, and there will be no room for flirtation. Tremendous discipline and hard work are needed. Why do you want to learn when you have already entrusted me with the investment and you can enjoy life visiting places and meeting people, which you seem to be extremely good at? Why have a dog and bark yourself?"

"We do not have any pets due to allergy issues. However, dogs do need to be carefully looked after, with frequent hugs and cuddles."

"I'm not too fond of these flirting talks and I will see you tomorrow at 7 am. You can have breakfast in the main office and on the first day I will join you there. After that, I will see you after your breakfast at 7.30 am in the main office."

"It is very considerate and accommodating of you," she replied. "However, I am not destitute, so I will join you at 7.30 am after my breakfast at home."

James met her the following morning, and she was exquisitely dressed. After one look at her, he told her it was an office and not to wear low-cut blouses and transparent dresses. He made Margaret fetch her a thin housecoat, with buttons from the neck to the knees, the same as he wore. Rose smiled and followed his instructions. Margaret and Clare smiled but would not tell their brother what not to do!

James discovered that Rose was very nervous when dealing with stocks but had an excellent telephone manner and she got all the details correctly. However, it took her more than double his time. He reassured her that she would do these tasks much faster with time and experience, and she was happy to hear his encouraging words.

James tried to train her, but by 5 pm she confessed she felt exhausted and began to appreciate his remarks about having a dog and barking oneself. She said she would not interfere and was not keen to learn anymore. She then left abruptly.

After dinner in Margaret's place, Mary, Nancy, Margaret, Clare and James discussed the situation.

"Dear James," said Margaret. "You seem to have inadvertently annoyed Rose this afternoon. She was in tears when she left."

"She is madly in love with you; I hope you realize that," said Clare.

"I am sorry if I upset her," he said. "When I train someone, I expect rapt attention, which was missing. I was annoyed and asked her: why have a dog and bark yourself? She asked me to invest for her, and she should focus on other things. She made a silly remark about not having any pets in her house due to allergy issues and that when one has a dog, it needs to be carefully looked after, with frequent hugs and cuddles. Funny though it may sound, I was annoyed with her flippant attitude. I felt she was not focused enough on trading."

"My darling, James," sighed Mary, "you are so bright on everything except when it comes to love! She has consistently indicated her interest, but like an idiot, you ignored the signs. So please apologize when you see her next and make peace."

James smiled but refused to accept.

After a few days, Rose called him to confirm the documents from BSL had arrived and he should come to her house to complete the formalities. Her family was expecting him and invited him to join them for lunch. She did not accept his refusal, and reluctantly, he agreed. He told her his dietary restrictions, to which she agreed after mocking him about it.

James reached her house, a 20-minute brisk walk away. It had an imposing entrance with security gates and a guard. The guard let him in after checking with Rose. He had to walk for another 20 minutes on a tree-lined driveway before he came to a palatial house with a roundabout at the front. Rose was waiting for him with Philip, her brother and Paula, his wife. After the usual greetings, Rose exclaimed,

"James, I did not realize you were walking. I would have

come to pick you up from your house."

"I like walking, and the walk up to this mansion was enjoyable. However, your chauffeur might drop me after I finish here."

They entered the house into a spacious entrance room and a vast assembly hall. Rose's parents and Jason, her younger brother, greeted him and after pleasantries, they all entered an enormous living room.

Rose's parents were very impressed with James, and his imposing personality and cinema star looks endeared him to all of them. The maid brought drinks, and James chose ordinary water without ice. Philip wanted all to sit and talk.

"Please do not regard my comments as rude," responded James. "I'd prefer to get on with the job, and when complete, we can sit down and chat. Where do we go, Rose?"

"Follow me," she said and took him to a vast office with all the modern typewriter facilities.

James read the letter and documents from BSL then completed the formalities, and said they would have to wait for further communications from BSL. He talked to Jason and found out his speciality subjects like physics, chemistry and mathematics, but he was not keen on becoming a medical doctor. Jason was good at English, and he was not eager to go to university. Journalism interested him most as a career.

"Jason, start writing small articles on areas of interest to youngsters like you. Then send them to local and national newspapers," advised James. "If the school has a magazine, send an article to your teachers to see how well you write. Even if they do not publish your articles, send them frequently and they will notice your name."

"I never thought of this," said Jason. "I'll make a start immediately."

"Please do not write critical reports but learn to praise the articles. You are at a young age of learning and not judging people or issues. Always be positive."

"May I send the articles to you first to check?"

"You may," replied James, "but I would only correct your spelling, etc. I would not change the subject matter or your expressions but keep your originality. You could drop in anytime at my place. Do you cycle and are you allowed to ride on the main roads?"

"I ride on the main roads and go to many of my friends living 5 to 6 miles from here. Your house, I understand, is less than a mile away. I will call you in a couple of days to fix a time to meet."

"That is fine with me. Rose? It is nearly noon. What time is lunch here?"

Just then the maid walked in and requested them to come to the dining room. There was a massive table with 12 settings but there were only seven that morning. The cook had prepared his vegetarian food without any garlic.

"Garlic is perfect for the heart and general health; why are you against it, James?" asked Philip.

"Mainly the smell. I have many quirks and I am a difficult person to live with. My mum would vouch for that."

After lunch, they all sat in the lounge and James told Jason to write something for him to read before going home. Jason left the room to do that.

"James," said Rose's mum, "you are the most modest person we have met in all these years, and it is more your style to put yourself down and praise others. I am sure your mum would be over the moon with your company. British people never liked garlic, but it has become a fad with the younger generation. I have seen you not taking wine or strong drinks except water. You must be very disciplined."

"Except on birthdays and Christmas," he replied. "I might drink a small measure of champagne. Otherwise, I do not take any drinks and eat modestly. I avoid junk food. I do not smoke. I have to focus on my work from 7 am to 10 pm, and keep my wits about me all the time. I avoid going to parties or eating food outside. Today is an exception for me to come for lunch and be away from trading. I need to go back soon."

"You are the exact opposite of me," laughed Philip. "I love to smoke cigars, drink and take drugs occasionally. I do not work or earn money and live on parental and ancestral income. My parents would dream of me being like you. We are like oil and water. We would never mix."

"I think you are too harsh on yourself, Philip," said Paula. "You could change a little bit to be more acceptable to all. James was obviously a model son."

"James," interjected Rose's mum. "No one in this house has ever spent time with Jason, advised him what to do and what not to do. Watching you both talk, Jason was so excited, please keep in touch with him."

"I shall. He can cycle to my place whenever we agree to meet. You have such a palatial mansion. Are you descendants of any royalty, please?"

"My great-great-great-grandfather was a descendant of King

Charles," she replied, "and the King bequeathed this property to us. As it is a listed building, maintenance is paid for by the government. We get invited to many formal Royal occasions. My grandfather was very irresponsible, spending the family fortune, smoking, drinking, and womanizing. My father steadied the ship, but he did not study in a college. We were three daughters; two passed away ten years ago due to cancer. My husband did not go to any university and we were not strict with Philip. Only Rose was the exception in studying well and managing the property and its assets. Her stunning looks get her many admirers, but she is not interested in any of them. Jason is mediocre in his studies, and I hope he builds a secure future with your guidance."

At that moment, Jason entered and handed over his report to James, who read it with great interest, smiling. He made only one correction and handed back the article to Jason, who was delighted with the glowing remarks and gave James a tight hug with tears in his eyes.

"You seem to have a very inflated opinion of my achievements," said James, addressing Rose's mum. "Journalism takes a good ten years of hard and dedicated work as a career. After that, pay could be inadequate, and he might have to work freelance. It isn't easy to get a secure job at the beginning of a career.

"If you have good contacts with a known journalist, he could be his understudy for a few years. He could also seek a PA job with an MP to research various issues, prepare speeches, and support the tour. He should be able to manage himself. I am sure he would not have to share the mortgage or living costs. He would have to watch out for pretty secretaries or even the female MP for whom he works for his frequent travels with late and long work hours.

"He could be a reporter for various TV channels and local or foreign news. He has a lot to choose from and has to play smartly. He would need a lot of guidance at this initial stage, and I am sure Rose would do her bit for the welfare of her dear brother!"

"I will play second fiddle after you, as you have a vast knowledge of these issues," she replied.

"James, you have given me tasks to find from my contacts in two areas," said Rose's mum, "and I am happy to have something to do to keep my mind active. It was our good luck we met you today. It was like a breath of fresh air to all of us. I think we shall have a short siesta. I hope to see you soon. Bye."

She and her husband left and Rose insisted on dropping him back, despite James opting for a good walk or a chauffeur to drive him. She thanked him for all his guidance to Jason and motivation to others, particularly to her mum. Rose had never seen her so talkative and enjoying herself.

"Please do come in to see her, as she does not travel."

So, he had to come to see her and all of them. She suggested that her transfer shows up in the BSL account in three days. James felt it was not necessary so quickly and planned after a month or so. Till then, they could each operate from their respective homes and give everyone a breather. Only Jason he would like to see, whenever he wanted. She smiled, dropped him off outside his house, and returned home, much to his surprise.

4
Slowly, slowly, catch the monkey

James traded for Rose. She was happy that she did not have to do anything. He was due to visit her house on Saturday for lunch. Mary, Margaret and Clare had daily discussions with Rose and were aware of his visit on Saturday. Unknown to James, Rose invited the three on Saturday to her place. When James arrived, he went to the lounge and was surprised to see his mum and sisters. He was also pleased to see Jason who told him,

"I sent the article to my teacher, the local paper, and an agent for the Children's Daily Telegraph. The teacher was happy to publish in the next month's bulletin; the local paper did not respond, but Fiona of the Daily Telegraph agreed to see and interview me on Tuesday at 5 pm here. Will you please arrive at least by 4 pm to help boost my spirits?"

Jason explained to the three ladies what had happened, and Rose filled in the missing bits.

"I am very proud of you, Jason," said James. "I would be delighted to be here. Think 2 out of 3 as positives and the remaining one as yet unknown. I'd like to have a mock interview with you, and we could spend some time after lunch on our own, is that ok?"

Jason hugged James with tears in his eyes and thanked him. James gave him a friendly pat. The maid announced that lunch was ready, and they all left for the dining room. As usual, the cook made special items for James, which surprised his mum and sisters. All enjoyed the food and the company and Mary told them about how they all met in London. Rose's mum and Paula were astonished how the three families and their two friends had bonded, with imminent marriages to take place. James chipped in to say that Rose's family were descendants of King Charles I. Rose's mum explained the details, and his mum and sisters were spellbound listening to her and were admiring the palatial settings in this fabulous house. After lunch, they all retired to the lounge.

"James," said Philip. "I have tried to cut down on smoking and drinking by 10% each week. Could you suggest something I could do to spend my time usefully? I'd be most grateful."

"Philip, I have some plans for you and Paula," replied James. "You should come to my place on Monday to check the suitability."

"James, you are a brother to me as well, please help us," said Paula.

"I spoke to two of my contacts," said Rose's mum. "The lady MP would be most interested to talk to Jason next Friday at 6 pm in her surgery. I feel you should accompany Jason with Rose, as she's known Rose since she was a toddler. The other contact is from DT as well, and he said that if it did not work out with Fiona, he would offer him a paid job as one of his assistants. What do you think, James? We were all happy about that, but you don't seem so sure?

"Jason would be in an intense work environment. If one of the assistants happened to bully him, Jason would not be able to report to your contact. It is better to decline it, even if it did not work out with Fiona. It is very early for him and there are more fish in the sea."

"You make more sense than any of us. Mary, you have a Solomon as your son. Did you realize that? I want to ask your son to marry Rose. What do you say?"

Mary hesitated. After talking to the girls, with tears in her eyes, she said that James was an adopted child in Calcutta and narrated the whole episode apart from before their adoption.

"As regards marriage, I would leave it to him to decide," she said.

"I would be delighted to marry James if only he would agree to it?" said Rose.

Philip and Paula both chimed in that they would be delighted.

"And I would be ecstatic," said Jason.

"Please calm down all of you," said James, "including Rose's mum. Your stunningly beautiful daughter is on top of Everest. She should be catching stars like PMs or a minister's son, an industrialist's son, or someone at a higher level. She should not - and you as her mother should stop her — be looking down and searching the gutter for a soul mate.

"My biological mother bore me as her second child. It isn't easy to get babies for adoption in India, and it was prohibitively expensive. My birth mother had already given her first baby for adoption, and when I was born, she did not want to see or hug me as she needed the money. I was known as Rama, and my parents were Shantha and Krishna, the elder brother of our friends Tara and her husband Rajesh, living close to us here. After four years, tragedy struck; four thugs entered our house, demanded money, and murdered my first adopted parents and two grans, but I was asleep upstairs and the thugs missed me. The adoption agency took care of me, and then my present mum and dad in Calcutta adopted me, which was the second time. They named me James.

"Rose's mum, you have an extraordinary lineage to be proud of, and where do I fit in? God has been considerate, given me wealthy parents, and sent me to an expensive school and what you see of me now is to their credit only. You also said that Rose had many admirers, and I am sure she would find a suitable one soon. I promise to be a brother to all from now to my dying day."

"English Kings had many bastard children, and these do not appear clearly in our lineage," replied Rose's mum. "It is all kept hidden for a cause to give us more support in our lives. I would not be mesmerized by descendants of King Charles I. What you are now is more important than what you were then. In our case, what we were then was more important than what we are now. James, you were too modest and told Rose to invest with other investors for a better return. She quite cleverly refused. You seem to have predicted 6% in a year, and you have exceeded that in 4 weeks. You have a very deprecating personality when you talk about yourself, but you are tremendously encouraging and motivating when it comes to others. Take a few days, spend some time alone with Rose and please get married soon. Let happiness flow in this house again through you, James."

Jason and James left for a few minutes to prepare for the interview on Tuesday. James wrote out a questionnaire to answer and follow - not to get too excited, speak slowly, not too fast, so that she could understand what he says.

"List the points in clear terms, say why you like journalism and what options you have. Try to behave as a bright boy and not as an adult. If you can write another article on a current topic concerning youngsters, please do so and show it to me. You can surprise her on that day."

Jason was so happy and told everyone about it.

"Rose's mum has all the answers," said Margaret. "Please be nice to Rose and wed her soon."

James smiled and agreed it would be soon after the sisters were married. Unknown to them, Rose heard it and so did Clare.

Rose's mum wanted to have a short siesta, so she and her husband left. Mary and the girls, together with James left for home as well. Rose dropped them off and did not say a word to anyone. James was surprised. Clare said that she and Rose had heard him say about marrying her after the sisters' weddings.

"Rose was so happy that you had finally agreed. She said her life was complete."

James laughed and told his mum that he might have to live with them after the wedding as he did not have a property of his own, so he was in a quandary. Mary said that was acceptable and they were not that far off from their house.

"I have an excellent solution to give a classy outlook to both your businesses," said James. "I have seen a big detached bungalow within the complex, and I think you both can leave the annexe and work from there. Also, mum and dad can stay with me to be close to your business, Margaret. They can give the house to Susan and Peter, needing separate accommodation."

"It is a beautiful idea," said Mary. "John was concerned about accommodation for Susan, and you have solved it. I'd like to talk to all the parents about holding a combined wedding within a month. I am sure Rose's mum would prefer a wedding in their palatial mansion, and she may not like to combine the wedding. Maybe I will ask her soon. With your marriage to Rose, she may agree to do anything."

"Mum, please ask Dennis to invite Rose and family, the six of them, for early lunch tomorrow to arrive at 10 am for a critical discussion with our clan and them. Tell them your suggestion, excluding Rose's wedding and including Rose's wedding. Rose's mum will respond clearly," said James.

Mary talked to Dennis, and he and Peggy agreed to the program.

Everyone invited Rose's mum, and she decided to come, stating the suspense of the discussion was too much for her. Dennis invited them to dinner that evening, and she accepted and promised to be there by 6 pm. It surprised the clan, and they assembled at Peggy's place by 5.45 pm. When Rose came with her family just before 6 pm, they gathered in the lounge, and the maid served drinks of their individual choice. Mary did all the introductions and background pieces of information for the benefit of Rose's mum, who replied,

"I am amazed at how you all met and stuck together as a clan from the stage of children at school in most cases. I am dying to know what today's discussion is?"

"I request the boy and girl to stand up when I call their names," said Mary. "Please oblige."

She then listed the couples who would be wed shortly and listed the six couples' names for everyone to recognize.

"All weddings within the clan. How wonderful for all the mums and dads!" said Rose's mum.

"The dates and location are issues," said Mary. "My suggestion is to hold it in one venue on the same date and time; a group wedding. I have more to say if the others in the clan agree?"

All the other parents agreed and were pleased with the simple solution.

"This is known as being on the same wavelength all the time. What is your next issue, Mary?" asked Rose's mum.

"It is a very delicate request. As my son, James, has agreed to marry your daughter Rose as you requested yesterday, would you like to join the group wedding or hold it separately? "

"We are all delighted that my daughter Rose is marrying her beau soon. I can see her cheeks getting red. Please give us a few moments to congratulate the young couple."

Everyone hugged the couple; Rose's dad was in tears and so were her brothers and Paula. Rose was crying too but controlled herself soon. James was smiling and enjoying the new family scenes. The clan was thrilled with the news, most unexpected they all remarked but very fitting for such a lovely boy and a stunning girl. They all were waiting for further comments.

"This fantastic news should follow with my 100% acceptance of Mary's proposal," said Rose's mum. "But at this stage, I can only agree with 50% of your request. All clan's weddings would have few outside guests. But we may have to invite several, mostly unknown to you all. One way to resolve this would be to have all the weddings in one setting and have a combined reception on the same date. After a few days, we might have a separate reception for Rose and James, with our other well-known contacts."

The whole clan clapped at the unique instant solution and

each hugged her warmly.

"I have a special request for Mary," she continued. "I want John and you to stay with us in our mansion from now on. I found your company stimulating, and James keeps my mind alert. I am sure he would run our estate and assets, along with Rose. I do not want him pining for you; hence, you stay with all of us here. Let all the married couples go to their respective chosen homes after the wedding."

"You have given us excellent news," said Mary joyfully, "and we will take your offer and stay with you all and give total support to James to focus on your estate management. This good news merits another. My daughter Susan does not have a house of her own, and John and I would leave the house to her to occupy her new/old place with Peter after her marriage."

Susan and Peter gave the parents hugs for the excellent wedding surprise present.

"We need to decide on the location, date, and time," said Mary. "The ball is in your court, Rose's mum."

"If I said a fortnight Friday from now, is it enough time for you all? My people will organize it, and if it is inconvenient, please let me know by tomorrow."

Mary spoke to all the parents and confirmed the date was most convenient. Each family had agreed to give money by check to the married couples as a present. Because the various Christian denominations and a couple of brides were Hindus, they would like to have a civil wedding and not a church wedding.

"I have decided to bear the total wedding costs for the day," said Rose's mum. "So, please increase your check amounts, as none of you would have to incur wedding and related expenses.

We would agree to a civil wedding as well."

The maid came to announce that lunch was ready, and they left for the dining room. After a sumptuous lunch and coffee, they went to their homes. Rose wanted James to stay on till dinner, and she agreed to drop him home by 10 pm.

Once the visitors left and her parents and brothers went for a siesta, she took James to her room. She wanted a kiss for all her pent-up feelings of several weeks. James confessed that she would be the first girl he had kissed.

"Loverboy, let me update you. You are my first kiss, despite being a stunning girl. I went to an expensive private girls' school up to 'A' levels. Then my brother Philip was worried about his sister. So, I had a private tutor and did my degree course at UCL by postal, as well as my Master's at the London Business School. So, no boys were allowed in this mansion and parties were few. Boys and men are not allowed to talk to me. If I was in Coventry, I could ride a white horse, like Lady Godiva!"

"Show me the house, please," he asked, "as I have a few requests to make."

"James, you are the monarch of all you survey from today. Let me show you, starting with the office."

It was a massive room with the latest IBM typewriter facilities for three people to work. The larger table was for her use and a similar one for her brother, which he never used and did not understand computers to help with the work. A smaller table was for any secretary to use from time to time. The large office for the secretary had all filing cabinets, printers, a photocopier, a few desks, and other small office furniture.

Her bedroom with the king-size bed was massive and had table lamps on both side tables. There was a good-sized walk-in closet, a standard size room for study with all up-to-date books, manuals, and the latest magazines, primarily for women, an enormous ensuite bathroom and a separate WC with a shower unit.

"Do you like what you have seen so far? And any comment on which side of the bed you want to sleep?"

"All brilliant so far and would not change your present arrangement. May I see the large bungalow by the side of this mansion?"

"My granddad built that apartment for the granny many years ago. The granny controlled the estate, and there were two office rooms, two rooms for her secretaries, and other facilities. Unfortunately, it has remained empty for years."

"I want to move the company premises of Margaret and Clare to this bungalow," he said, "saving me time to travel there to oversee their business as well. They would pay a rent of £750 per month. My mum is the CFO for finances, and she would find it convenient with their premises here. Once they move here, I want you to be CEO of marketing. You would draw a salary of £1,000 per month."

"James, you must have planned this for weeks! If you were planning to marry me, why did you delay all this time?"

"You are irresistible, but my lineage stopped me from opening my heart to you. Since your mum changed my mind about being a neglected adopted child a week ago, I agreed to wed you. Till then, I thought you deserved someone much better than me."

"You are the best for me, and I am delighted about that. What else have you planned, please tell me?"

"I want to modify the garden, but it could wait until the girls move in. I need to find jobs for Philip and Paula. I need to know their skills and what they like to do."

They entered her bedroom and she could not resist further kisses. He responded and promised there would be more to follow after the wedding.

It was tea time. The cook in his house knew how to make filter coffee for James. Rose said the cook could work under the chef in their mansion. Rose told her mum about the bungalow, the monthly rental income, and her becoming CEO marketing monthly. James would also like to talk to Philip and Paula later about suitable jobs. After coffee, tea and cakes, James wanted to speak to Paula and Philip privately. He went with Paula first to one of the rooms.

"Paula, please tell me your likes and what you would like to do?"

"I did not go to university as I was a mediocre student. I was a secretary's assistant, but I lost my job within two years due to many errors in my typing. After that, I got married to Philip and never needed to work. I am happy to do simple filing in the office and answer the phones."

"With such limited skills, I can see a job as a clerical assistant for filing, copying, and telephone answering services," he said. "Your salary would be £200 monthly. There would not be any threat of sacking, and you would report to two bosses. Would you be interested?"

"I am delighted and would try to satisfy them. It is a breakaway from my monotonous life now."

She hugged and kissed James on his cheeks. James thanked her and requested to send Philip to the room.

"Philip, please let me know your skills and what you would like to do as a job?"

"I never studied and did not go to university. I did not manage anything because I indulged in smoking, drinking, drugs, and womanizing till I married Paula. I did some accounts, but my mind was not on the job. If I'm honest, I would not give a job to a person like me."

"I have to think of the family," responded James, "and you are the elder son. I would request you to be the manager of the Estate upkeep, referring to the gardens only. You will be paid £250 monthly and report to me. No drinking, smoking, or taking drugs would be permitted and lead to immediate sacking. If agreeable, please let me know. None of the others needs to know our discussions and the terms of the job."

"I am very grateful to you, James, and I have cut smoking and drinking by 80% already. I have not taken drugs for over three years. I thank you for the confidential discussion."

They returned to join the others. It was nearly time for early dinner. After dinner, James saw Rose in her room and after a parting kiss, she dropped him home but did not go inside. James and Mary went to the annexe and talked to Margaret and Clare. He updated them on all aspects, including the salaries but not the confidential discussions with Philip. They all regarded it as a very productive day. The sisters wanted to gossip about his meeting with Rose, but Mary said it was a long day for James, and they all needed a good sleep. Reluctantly, the sisters agreed and allowed them to leave. Before leaving, James told the three of them never to reveal the sister's relationship to Rose or anyone there, despite his relationship with Rose.

"She is very confidential; you could tell her later but not now."

The following week, Rose wanted him to work from her place to discuss the modifications to the bungalow. She arranged with the sisters to discuss their opinions later that evening after 5 pm. James saw Rose with her mum in the office.

"This week, the return is slightly lower, any reason?" asked Rose.

"My original trading conditions set out returns varying from losses to gains to 1% per week. These may appear small, but over a year, it is substantial," he replied.

"It is a valuable lesson to learn and follow Rose," said her mum. "For me, even 1/2% weekly is a significant return."

James went to the office and took the desk adjacent to Rose, despite her insisting he took her desk. He spent an hour arranging his files and folders. Then, he logged into BSL and started trading on the clan's accounts. James did not want to charge any commission for the families in the group. They reluctantly agreed.

"What a heart for a child adopted twice, who never tasted his mother's breast milk or had cuddles, except from his adopted parents. Rose, you are blessed to wed him," said her mum. "But, please make sure you never argue or quarrel with him or hurt him with harsh words."

"I would never do, mum. I promise all of you."

"In South India," said James, "the mother and father are Amma and Appa, respectively. For me, mum and dad are the ones from my adoption. So, you both are Amma and Appa to me from today. Amma, I will take your advice and inform them."

James informed all the four families in the clan that no

deductions were necessary for his monthly expenses. They were insisting on paying something, but he refused to accept. Finally, at 5 pm, his mum came with Clare and Margaret. James discussed modifications to their studios and the contractor, who had experience working with other artists, and noted all the requirements. He was able to suggest many, which both of them accepted. By 6 pm, they all returned home. James told them that he would be working for free for the families in the clan and the girls on their investments.

"A few days ago, you refused a monthly salary as you would make a 10% commission on our investments, and today you confirm not taking any commission," said Margaret.

"How will you meet your expenses?" asked Clare.

"On commissions from other investors only. I will survive, do not worry," he assured them.

There was a call from Dennis, the business magnate in the clan at that time. He said he had confirmed with the other investors in the family group, and their unanimous decision was to deduct 2% for commission for James, and it would be their wedding present to the new couple. They would not accept any refusal. So saying, he said good night, and he put the phone down.

Mary advised James to accept gracefully as half of it belonged to Rose! She gave a motherly hug, and they left for home.

The following morning, the families of the whole clan were busy with the wedding on Friday, and there was a lot of excitement. All details collected were needed for the civil marriage, like passports, birth certificates, deed poll, addresses, etc. By agreement, James and Rose did not see each other till the wedding day.

Mary said that none of the staff and headteachers from the private school could attend the wedding due to the summer holidays. They all had gone abroad. So they would give them a party in a month. Dennis and Keith felt that as they had lived abroad, they did not have anyone close to call for the wedding, and, if allowed, they would join the party in a month.

On Friday, they all met in the large living room of the family mansion at 11 am. The Council's Registrar to carry out the civil marriages was there with five assistants occupying separate tables for each bride and groom. The Registrar was officiating Rose's wedding with James. The Registrar and his assistants finished all marriages and issued certificates within an hour. All couples had to kiss for a group photo, but Priya and Asha hugged their husbands without kissing, as Indian girls were too shy to show their affection in public!

They all had a fabulous buffet lunch in the vast dining room. All couples cut cakes, all three tiers, and after concise speeches, they returned to their respective homes. James's parents stayed in the mansion from that evening. After all the other families had left, Rose's and James's family met in the living room with coffee for a chat.

"We thank you, Rose's mum," said Mary, "for a splendid civil marriage arrangement, lunch, cakes, etc. The whole ceremony went very smoothly, and all were delighted. It was inexpensive too for all of us except you! We are happy that James has become your son-in-law, which you wished for some time."

"I feel I have completed a big project to everyone's satisfaction," replied Rose's mum. "The cost was less than an average bride's family would incur, and we had six marriages performed. My dream of weeks since seeing James for the first time has come true. I feel now it is like a shot in my arm to have him live here with us. I am sure he and Rose would be the most beautiful couple for years to come and bless us with children to run around this house soon. We all should have a short siesta and meet again in a couple of hours."

They all retired to their rooms, with a maid taking James's mum and dad to their room.

Once in Rose's bedroom, she and James noticed the fragrance of scents, roses, and other flowers. The was a plate full of fruits and jugs of milk and fruit juices to take. Rose hugged James and wanted him to consummate the marriage. He calmed her down and told her, "Slowly, slowly, catch the monkey." She made him lead her and they had a fantastic time, which neither had experienced before. They set the alarm for 90 mins, and both were in a deep sleep within minutes. When the alarm went off, they rushed, had showers, and only then did James realize he did not bring his suitcases with him. He did not have any change of clothes. He rang the house and asked the maid to pack three cases of clothes and bring them here. James wore his wedding clothes and met all others downstairs. They had a good laugh, and Rose's mum told Rose it was her job to make sure that James had what he wanted available immediately from now on. In 30 minutes, the cases had arrived, and Rose, with a maid, went to arrange his clothes in the walk-in cupboards. The maid came down to ask James to see madam upstairs. James went up, changed to his evening clothes and came down with Rose to re-join them. The chats continued for an hour or so. The night dinner was very light. All went to bed very early, which suited the newly wedded couple too!

5
Neither a borrower
nor a lender be

The following day, James got up to see Rose already up and getting things ready for him in the office. She placed the papers nicely on the table, and all folders were kept handy. Rose had told the maid to follow the tasks from now on. Next, Rose and James had breakfast together, as it was too early for others to join. Once they finished, the maid brought exceptional percolated coffee to James and Rose in the office room.

"From today, Rose," he said, "all new and old investors will deal with you only, to set up accounts with BSL and all procedures. I will only see their investments and details of their performances. Thanks for the early morning preparations. I need a few things from you as soon as possible."

He asked her to find the total figure of the various household costs, utilities, credit, debit cards, etc. She studied the request and said that the marriage was not even fun for a day!

The two venture capitalists visited the new premises and what dazzled them most was the Chief Marketing Officer, Rose, with her stunning looks. In a typical Indian fashion, she did a namaste, and on that day, she was wearing a Saree. They were impressed with the four reproduction paintings and the four portraits. They credited £20,000 for the reproduction paintings and £12,000 for the portraits.

Rose's mum happened to hear the prices, and she asked all of them to come to one room. She had six reproduction paintings, each valued at £20,000, and ten portraits, each valued at £10,000. She advised Rose not to accept the money as these two seemed like novices, and she would arrange to sell these at prices she quoted. The two venture capitalists had a long chat and agreed to pay £120,000. Rose's mum told them about being descendants of King Charles I. They were very impressed and apologized for trying to trick the young girls. Rose's mum said they should not have any commission, as the buyers pay 15% to the auctioneers. So, they gave a further check of £30,000 and agreed to operate for no commission. The two venture capitalists ordered six reproduction paintings, five portraits, and three nudes, portraits, two females and one male. The subjects would dictate the level of nudity they would like. Rose insisted that no one should accompany the people, and the artists would indicate the date, time, and duration to complete. The two venture capitalists left, thanking Rose's mum.

James felt it was a most beneficial day for the girls. The girls thanked James for moving their studios here. They had never expected an income of £75,000 each in such a short time, and Rose's mum should have half of it. Rose remarked that her mum should be the CMO, and she would be her assistant, which her mum refused both the payments and the new post as CMO. She said nude portraits usually merit £20,000 to £30,000 each and be careful before accepting payments. Rose said that she would never take money without consulting her mum. Margaret and Clare offered to do a free portrait of Rose's mum solo and with her husband. She was thrilled and said,

"I saw the four reproductions. As regards reproductions, Clare was excellent when multiple characters were present. Margaret was better when only one character was involved.

Same regarding portraits."

She felt that Margaret should do the solo portrait and Clare the family one. Both the girls were happy at the beautiful assessment of their skills and the separation of their tasks.

"James," said Rose, "taking the current and future level of all staff, I estimate a total cost of £44,000 per year.

James felt they needed a reserve of £0.5 million and their interest to fund their yearly cost without worrying about the future.

After dinner, the family met in the lounge and Rose updated them on the day's events, income, etc. Philip and Paula were happy with the day and admired the paintings and the portraits. Philip agreed to spend the week with a gardener to improve the girls' garden.

"I have one suggestion to make," said James, "and hope you all agree. All of us, the whole clan group, should meet every Sunday at lunchtime in someone's house by rotation. And, I would like the girls to eat here on weekends."

"That is a splendid idea," said Rose's mum, "and I expect you, Rose, to organize that."

"I will do that tomorrow, mum."

After an hour, they all retired to their bedrooms.

Rose talked first to Dennis and Peggy. They agreed with the concept of meeting but suggested meeting in his place to alternate with Rose's. All others were agreeable to the two locations. Rose's mum agreed that it was the most prudent solution.

Barclays Bank PLC had given them a mortgage years ago,

and the manager was well known to Rose's mum. Rose opened a Trust Fund for the mansion expenses so that all winnings were credited to that Fund account only. James followed his trading pattern.

Rose got all the information James wanted, and it made for dismal reading. The family was not wealthy for all the mansion's grandeur and had only meagre savings and investments. They had already overdrawn on to the limit of £30,000. The mortgage on the estate was £600,000, and no one had any income. It was surprising that the bank had not pulled the rug from under them so far. It was like Rome burning, but Nero was playing the flute! Rose's mum wanted to know his solution.

"Gamble with stocks," James quipped. "I need to study the form."

Then he abruptly left them and went to his room to look at papers.

Unfortunately, the details of penny stocks in the USA or South America were not listed. So, he telephoned one of his contacts in the USA to send some highly volatile stocks with prices, to fax him in the night to trade the next day. As the East Coast was five hours behind, and it was 2.30 pm there, in 30 minutes, the contact faxed 12 stocks with prices and how they traded the previous four days.

The following day, James decided not to trade in overseas stocks, due to delays in money transfers, tax deductions at source on gross winnings, and variable exchange rates. He talked to Rose about penny share trading, the risks and the benefits. Finally, he gave her a stock market journal to read about it. Rose read and felt most was above her head and would go by James's judgment, which had been excellent, judging from the bride James had chosen!

Rose wanted to know about trading in penny shares. James started explaining that assuming the stock valued 1p, one invests £1,000, hoping the price would rise, and sometimes they went as high as 90p, which meant investment became £90,000, which was a rare scenario. One had to invest in many such shares, hoping some would appreciate. Assuming one buys twenty different stocks and only one stock increases in value to 25 p, but the rest are below 1p, then one's gain is only £6,000 (25,000-19,000) and £19,000 below 1p, one has to hold on till they recover to 1p so that one could sell the stock to recover the money. Also, if the share value goes to 90p, one may not be able to sell all the shares because there may not be enough buyers, and it would mean selling as much as possible immediately and selling the rest later. But by then, the share price could plummet to 1p. Rose wanted James to do what he thought was best for the family.

Following stringent rules and gambling on losing up to £20,000, he invested in penny shares and made £50,000 after a week. James always ensured that the return for other investors averaged daily 1/8%, which they all appreciated. He traded for several weeks on penny shares.

James, Rose, and her mum met one morning in the Trading office, and after the maid delivered coffee and closed the door, James explained,

"Amma, I had traded dangerously for two months and had diced with danger. However, I managed to accumulate a profit of £750,000 in the mansion Trust Fund. I have paid off the outstanding overdraft amount of £30,000, and today, I want to pay off £550,000 towards the mortgage. It would look nice if you talk to the Manager of Barclays Bank PLC about this re-payment."

Both Amma and Rose hugged and kissed him.

Amma then talked to the delighted manager, who asked the reason for this wealth, whether they had won the lottery? She let James explain to him. The manager was so flabbergasted that he wanted James to look after his investments. James took that as a joke and escaped any commitment. Instead, he told Amma and Rose that he might take the Bank Manager as an investor, hoping he would not retire within 20 years to take good care of them.

"Rose," said her mother, "I am very relaxed after many years of anxiety. James has removed the financial yoke of all these years."

"I have to play this game for a few more months," he said, "and this time I would not be stressed. I would play in a relaxed way. I need to save £1.5M in the trust fund for various expenses incurred for the mansion house. This amount would set us for life. I will start tomorrow."

"Rose, you need to reward James very well. Please agree to whatever he requests. All he desires you should meet, and as a dutiful wife, you should please him with whatever he wants."

"Mum, you want me to give him an open check?"

"Yes, darling. Just grin and bear it. He has removed a significant calamity and brought peace to all of us."

"Whatever you dictate, mum! James, what do you wish to have? Name your desire, my heartthrob, please!"

"All relations, including Amma, are relatively young," he replied. "I feel we should have two children and close the chapter! You would have a lot of people to dote on the children. Nothing else I need! I hope you will think about it carefully and let me know in due course."

"How obedient do you want me to be to your wishes, lover boy? Do you want to go upstairs now, or do you wait till tonight? I was thinking about the same thing but did not have time to mention it. I have a similar opinion, so you have the most willing partner."

"Hilarious, Rose!" he laughed. "I am in no rush, and I can wait for a few hours to carry out our mission!"

"I am glad you both have responded well," said Amma. "Rose, you must know my aunt had twins, and it misses one generation. Yours is next, just to let you know."

"Thanks, mum, for your blessings!"

James realized he had about £30,000 in penny shares of no value in the BSL Trading account. Any faint-hearted person would have quit trading on penny shares. He risked another £20,000 to recover the £30,000. That day he made £25,000. After dinner, when all met in the lounge, Amma told everyone how James had made a lot of money on investing highly risky shares and paid off the overdraft and most of the mortgage. All were highly appreciative and thanked James. Amma did not elaborate on other discussions. Rose and James had a particular commitment to fulfil when all retired for bed, and they got on with the task merrily.

Several months went by and James had added £1 million to the trust fund. At the same time, he had £38,000 locked up in penny shares with a total value of less than £20.00. In another two months, he saved a further £300,000, and the Trust Fund had £1.5 million, enough to meet his target set initially. Slowly, James recovered £38,000, locked in penny shares, and quit trading. Amma and Rose were pleased and decided to keep this information confidential.

They were all meeting as planned and on one Sunday after dinner when all the family was present, Mary suggested that all should update on developments for each family.

"We were delighted with our daughters, Priya and Asha," said Peggy. "They have retained their South Indian upbringing but blended nicely with Western culture."

"All credit goes to Tara and Rajesh," added Dennis. "Russel and Trevor manage the two businesses with their spouses and they are better than what we had abroad. I must compliment James in returning growth of 10% so far in ten weeks of trading. I have never seen such a good return in all these years. This bonanza is to all investors present here."

"Debbie and Arthur, with their spouses, are managing the farms, admirably staying at home," said Keith. "They have appointed very able supervisors, and visiting the farm was not required. As a result, our incomes had also gone up."

"As Dennis said," added Joe, "We appreciate the best investment returns so far."

"We are glad Liz and Arthur are helping you, Joe, and Keith very well," said Nancy. "Susan and Peter are fine, and they enjoy the freedom in their new, surprise wedding gift, house."

"Margaret will update you all," said Jeff, "which we are waiting to hear. We also thank you, James, for our excellent return on investments."

Clare updated them on the work they had done with the reproduction paintings of Grand Masters and the four portraits. She also told of their future workload, including the new assignments on paintings of three nudes, two females and one male! Margaret updated their income on how the two venture capitalists tried to short-change them, paying only £50,000 and how Amma got involved, and they coughed up £150,000 with no commission charges in the future. All appreciated the skill of Amma and the prudent decision by James to move their studios to the mansion. Margaret said that she would do a portrait of Amma and Clare said she would do Amma and Appa, which would be FREE.

"I have to give news of sensational financial developments arising from James's trading," said Amma.

She narrated all from the amount of mortgage, overdraft, and near bankruptcy level to how James earned a phenomenal amount by gambling, taking sensible precautions, and paid back all overdraft, 95% of the mortgage, and enough money to cover all mansion expenses for years to come. "

"We are so lucky to have him and regard him more as a son. I did not want to tell anyone till today. I kept Mary in the dark for months."

"We are pleased that James solved the financial burden on the mansion," said John.

"And from the shoulders of Amma and Appa," said Mary.

"I have good news to share with all of you," said Rose. "James and I decided to have a couple of children soon, with you all young. My mum told me that her aunt had twins, and the general concept is it would miss a generation. However, the doctor said it was incorrect and had tested me on the 11th week. He confirmed twins, not identical but fraternal."

Starting with Amma, they all rushed to hug her and it took about 30 minutes to finish. Mary said similar reasoning might apply to other couples, and they should all get busy tonight! On that happy note, they all left for their homes.

"Rose, I am so happy about the twins," said Amma. "James, you wanted two children; you may end up with four!"

"Please, do not even joke. The last time you talked of twins, I ended up carrying twins! So let us see what is in store for us."

They retired to bed but James was so excited he couldn't sleep. They wanted to choose the names. James gave her consent to select the names she liked for the babies. Rose wanted a single-syllable name, Ann for a girl and Ben for a boy. James loved her selections. As they would not be identical twins, other choices were unnecessary. With a happy frame of mind, they both slept peacefully.

Soon, the other five couples announced their pregnancies with imminent births of babies, including twins, in the following twelve months, and the whole group was excited. Still, Rose did not know about the relationship between Margaret and Clare. The families were preparing for the new arrivals. James had ensured they all had good returns, totalling 40% in 6 months, the most unexpected by all of them. They felt the extra income would come in handy for having a different maid/childminder for the babies' mother.

Rose delivered the twins as expected on the predicted date, and it was a natural birth. The first was a girl, 8lb 5 oz, 17 in long, with blonde hair, lovely dimples, a small mouth, blue eyes, a very doll-looking girl. After 40 minutes, the boy was born, 8lb 2 oz, 18 in, very long fingers and toes, brown hair, aquiline nose, and brown eyes. They were named Ann and Ben. Amma and Appa were so thrilled to see the kids. However, the maid and the childminder were so busy and the children were demanding more milk, the boy would not release the nipples and Rose had to remove him forcibly. Rose looked so tired, and all were feeding her the most nourishing food to build up her strength and breastfeed the babies. For a few weeks, James had to sleep in the guest room so that the childminder could sleep in the main bedroom. James rarely talked to Rose, and all could see the constant demands made by the twins on all the adults.

James felt he had more time to focus on trading, and he was able to get a slight improvement on the weekly returns to 2%. However, Amma felt he should relax more if Rose needed him urgently and not get occupied with trading too much.

After dinner one Sunday, they sat in the lounge for a discussion.

"We have not been able to alternate dinner locations with Dennis and Peggy due to the twins," said Amma. "We might have to meet here for some months because Rose can come down for a few minutes and show the twins to you all here."

Just then, Rose and the maids brought the twins in. They could all see that Rose was thoroughly exhausted, but the twins were looking here and there and laughing. Ann seemed well behaved when Rose lifted the children, but Ben was looking for the breasts for feed and she had to excuse herself and go upstairs to feed the twins.

All appreciated how the girl was different from the boy, even though they were twins. They provided a conversation piece for all for nearly an hour. All the pregnant mothers attended the clinics for periodic checks with their husbands when needed. Starting with two months, the birth of each child should follow for the next eight months.

A few weeks went by and the twins were getting bigger, but their desire to feed also increased. Amma advised Rose to breastfeed for one year, maybe two years, but start solid foods after six months. All this was to improve the twin's immunity from various infections. Liz's baby was due first, followed by Priya, then Asha, Debbie, and finally Susan. They decided to hold the Sunday meetings in the house where a baby was born and skip Dennis's house, and later on, even skip Rose's place, as the twins would be old enough to take them to the other's house. Rose had to install tiny metal gates as the twins started crawling after four months.

A few weeks went by and Amma wanted a private chat with James and Rose. She came after feeding the twins.

"James," she said, "I have a suspicion you know a lot of things, which you only reveal as necessary. I saw Margaret and Clare walking in their garden, holding hands and at one stage kissing. Are they in a lesbian relationship?"

"How very interesting," said Rose. "Bare it all, lover boy?"

"It is highly confidential," replied James, "and even aunt Nancy did not suspect, despite Clare coming to her house for several years and attending all functions."

He then narrated all that happened and asked them not to even mention it to the girls that both of them knew.

"So now all in our group know except you and your family here," he added.

"So, you were very crafty to get the annexe in Dennis's house and the bungalow with private studios for the artists," said Amma.

"I have seen them going out with you, Peter and Liz. Was it to stop outsiders guessing and gossiping?" asked Rose.

"Precisely, my darling. They should think the girls have boyfriends, and no one benefits from us being brothers. I try to advise them what to do from time to time."

He then went on to explain, comparing his background with Clare and how she had suffered more.

"It was unfortunate to hear, and we will not make it a point of conversation whenever we meet. Kudos to you, James, for being such a devoted brother to Margaret and Clare and son to Nancy!" said Amma.

One of the twins started crying, and the maid came down to ask Rose to go up. So, the conversation ended, much as they would have liked to continue for a few more minutes. Within minutes, Rose came down to say the babies were asleep and maybe Ben needed mum's cuddle.

"Now I am all ears to know more about my sisters!"

"When I was young," said Amma, "a girl in our school belonging to a higher social class felt strange, as she said she was comfortable with girls and did not want any relationship with men, and her friends or family would not agree with her. They thought she needed psychiatric treatment, but it would mean admission to a lunatic asylum in those days. So, her parents forcibly married her very young. She fought against them, but with her elder brothers siding with her parents, she endured the wedding, and she was frightened of the first night and consummating the marriage.

"The due hour came; he was already undressed and tried to pull her to bed. She told him about her desire to be with a woman and not a man. It annoyed him and he ridiculed her to check what a man can offer before deciding on a downward trend! As he pulled her violently, she pulled out a 9-inch knife, which she had hidden in her dress, slashed both his hands and threatened to inflict damage downwards!

"After wrapping his hands with two kerchiefs, he quickly dressed, shouted, and left the room. No one came to see her that night. Her parents were very embarrassed, and her brothers wanted to follow the custom of honor killing, which his parents disagreed with. A young relative of hers specialized in Psychiatry and had a clinic in Croydon. He convinced her parents to let him treat her, and he would take care of all her expenses. They wanted to say, 'Good riddance to her and felt it was their God sent a gift to have her cousin to take her away from them.

"She never saw her parents again. Her cousin knew about lesbian tendencies in all the societies but never openly admitted them except for Gay relationships between men. He told her she could work as a nurse in his clinic with a handsome salary. She passed various exams through postal facilities and attended evening classes. She wrote a book about her experiences and became very famous. Now she has her own office with a secretary, her lesbian partner. She was able to get some MPs to acknowledge the facts about lesbian relationships, and from then on, the attitudes have started to change."

"That's very exciting, mum, you have so many varied experiences, you should write a book."

"I do not think people's perceptions have changed significantly despite any legislation," said James. "The attitude of acceptance is still rigid and one of intense dislike. That is why I am protective of the girls, and the whole group has agreed to shield them where possible. Even the staff working for the girls do not know about their relationship."

"We promise to do the same," confirmed Amma.

It was time to turn in for bed. The three left, with James going to the spare bedroom. A few weeks rolled by and Liz delivered a baby boy, a younger brother for Ann and Ben.

Nancy and Jeff's household was very busy with the new arrival.

Margaret and Clare came to Rose's place for dinner that weekend. After dinner, they were in the lounge for discussion.

"I am thinking of hiring two lady and male bodyguards, only for those days when the models arrive for nude portraits," said James.

"Why bodyguards for women models?" asked Clare.

"Why don't we see the women models and then decide about bodyguards?" suggested Amma. "What dangers are you worried about, James?"

"If the sisters were to go near them to adjust the coverings or position them before painting, they might hug them and move to compromise, then the bodyguards should help. More important for a male model."

"It is possible," said Amma, "but the models may not like bodyguards to view their bodies."

"Maybe, it is better to mention to the VCs and let them tell the models about what not to do," replied James, "and if they ignore it, then the deposit of £5,000 would not be returned with consequential loss of the contract. The bodyguards for the male and female models would wait outside the studio to help with an emergency."

"Thank you, James, for taking so much care about our safety," said Clare.

When the two lady models arrived, they were very sophisticated women and smiled at the conditions. They did not expect to see two attractive very young, artists. They admitted the need to guard for such situations. Margaret took the younger of the two models to her studio, and Claire took the older one.

Despite their ages, both wanted the full-frontal view, and without any inhibitions, they positioned themselves on a settee. The need to adjust their clothing did not arise!

Both worked for two hours and gave the models a break for an hour for comfort and lunch. Both artists then worked for two hours and finished by 5 pm. The girls used a sizeable magnifying mirror to see the various features clearly as the models were at a distance on the settee. The models left to return the next day.

After two weeks, the venture capitalists came to see the completed portraits. James, Rose, and Amma also came. All were impressed and very pleased with the so-natural-looking painting. More importantly, the models were amazed that such young artists could do so well. To the surprise of the venture capitalists, each paid the artist £50,000, saying their lovers had promised to pay £50,000 and advised the venture capitalists to sell it to them soon. It was most unexpected for all, including Amma. Only five of them were there, and Amma hugged both girls and blessed them for more glory to come their way. In their excitement, both girls hugged and kissed each other. When they realized, what they had done, they were ashamed and nearly in tears apologizing to James.

"I am glad you both kept it secret so long, which was highly commendable," he said. "Move on from now as if nothing had happened."

His comments made them cry, and Amma gave a hug to both. She then explained what she saw a few weeks ago and her talks with James. She also told them about her friend and coping many years ago.

"We thank you for such consideration and will not cross the line drawn by our brother James," said Clare and Margaret agreed.

"Tomorrow, the male model is due to come," said James, "and Amma suggested that Clare do his portrait when Margaret does Amma's solo portrait."

Both the girls agreed and left.

The next day, in the mid-20s, the male model came, and the venture capitalists explained the rules and precautions to take. He smiled and agreed to stand like a Michaelangelo. Clare told him that she would use the sizeable magnifying mirror to enhance facial and specific features for his portrait. She would not tolerate rude jokes and comments, please.

In four weeks, she completed his portrait. The usual people were there for the viewing. He boasted about his physique and body shape. He said it was better than even a Michaelangelo sculpture! The model was a heartthrob of his older wealthy girlfriend. He was her toy boy. By special permission, he brought her on condition only they, both with the artist, would view the painting later so that no one knew her identity. As she was so excited to see it, she gave Clare £60,000 on the spot and took the portrait. The venture capitalists had approved her actions. The lady mentioned that she had good contacts with a few museum officials who might pay upwards of £80,000. She promised to introduce some clients to Clare soon, directly not through the venture capitalists.

Later that evening, James told the girls that their company could trade with anyone, and venture capitalists happened to be one of the contacts and not exclusive. The girls wanted to invest £50,000 each with James, who told them to contact Rose.

6

It won't be sunny every day!

Tara announced that Priya had delivered a baby girl, and all were very happy. One more sister for Ann and Ben. The girls modernized their studios, kitchen, bathrooms, bedrooms and living rooms. As the workload increased, they had two more security people to guard the studio as the value of the portraits had soared. These changes took two months to complete. They wanted a modern Bar-B-Q set up in their garden to hold frequent parties. James was not happy with that because the twins were walking by now, and controlling them even with the help of maids was not easy.

The principal gardener sorted out the Bar-B-Q setup, but his assistant was not that bright. One afternoon, Rose was in the garden lying down and Amma was pruning the rose plants nearby and talking to Rose. James was near but watching the young assistant. He was lighting a kerosene burner, which was quite heavy. No one knew what exactly happened. There was an explosion and James fell flat on Rose, covering her face with both hands. The splash of burns fell on James's back and hands and the heavy burner was thrown high and impacted on James's spine, cutting the skin with blood oozing out of the spine area.

The principal gardener covered James with one of the blankets, smothered the flames and covered the burner, which was still burning. Amma immediately called for an ambulance, which came in ten minutes. Rose slightly moved the blanket to breathe, but Amma asked her not to turn or move as James was severely wounded. The paramedics saw the extent of the damage and burns sustained by James, but Rose had escaped totally. They prized out the heavy burner body and could see the blood oozing out and how it damaged the spinal column. It took them an hour to attend to his wounds; they lifted him gently and put him on a stretcher, face down. He was unconscious all this time.

Rose got up and the medics praised James for saving his wife's stunning face from any burns. His hairs had charred and the shirt got burnt 90%, and they could see the marks on the skin due to the burns. The whole group assembled in tears as they saw James wounded and unconscious. Amma wanted to know the effects of spinal cord injury. The medic refused to comment, saying the consultant would decide. Rose wanted to go with them, but the doctor advised her to come after three hours, not before. The assistant did not suffer any injury as the damage happened to James in front. He got up quickly and was sorry that he was responsible. The gardener suggested that maybe some water had got mixed with the kerosene and caused the explosion. The assistant must have filled the burner with water thinking it was a bottle of kerosene!

John and Mary suppressed their tears and told Rose not to cry as all would be ok. She should take care of the twins with the assistance of the maids. Peggy promised to stay and help Mary. Rose, Amma, Robert and Susan went to the hospital as none had seen James so helpless in all these years. The consultant told them that the impact on the spinal cord was severe, and he was waiting for some tests. He said that James was slowly regaining his consciousness and his first words were: "How's Rose?" They could not control their tears.

Rose asked whether he would walk normally, but the consultant would not comment. The specialist for spinal cord injury was due in an hour, and he would decide on the prognosis. The consultant felt they should leave now and come the next day by 9 am to know further. The specialist would also be there, and all the results for the tests he would recommend would be available in the morning. Amma advised returning home. Rose was pestering the consultant to give her some idea of the prognosis. He said there were good and bad outcomes. James would have all his faculties, including brain function. The dire situation was if James would be unable to walk unaided due to spinal cord damage and they would know more by tomorrow morning. James should have recovered more, had some food, and would be able to talk to them when they turned up.

Amma spoke to the consultant and arranged for family quarters with one extra room with all facilities so that an adult could stay if needed. Amma told the consultant about James and her family background. She said he needed the best medical cover at all times.

They all left with Rose inconsolable. Amma told her the twins needed her, and the hospital would take care of James. Rose then calmed down and started thinking of the twins. They were still on breastfeeds and would have missed one feed. Rose was worried about the twins immediately.

When they reached home, the whole clan joined them. Amma told them all the developments except the prognosis about unaided walking, and they would know more the following day after the spinal cord specialist sees all the test results. These words satisfied the clan, and they returned home. Despite the most worrying hours of her life, for the first time, the need to take good care of the twins and tiredness made Rose sleep soundly, and strangely the twins slept soundly without crying for a feed in the night.

The following day, the same four went to the hospital. Rose had arranged for the babies to be brought to the hospital after 4 hours for their feed. They found a smiling James lying on the bed but strapped with a wide, tight belt. The doctor explained that he should not move sideways to damage the injured spinal cord, and it would take four to five days to mend. After that, James could move with ease. With the tilting bed, he was more upright. Finally, the specialist spinal consultant took Rose and Amma to his room.

"I have mixed news regarding James's prognosis," he said. "All the tests indicate his mental and brain faculties are 100% intact and normal. However, he cannot walk unaided due to the spinal cord injury. It would mean he can use either a stick, a walking frame, or a wheelchair. Since he has a lot of determination, he would not be in a wheelchair. With time he may also walk unaided after a year or so, but you should never let him do any physical work.

"The burns on his back and hands will mend in a couple of months, but the scalding on top of the head and loss of hair will never come back. James may have to start wearing a wig for the rest of his life. I was amazed by James on two counts; firstly, his tremendous love for you by preventing even slight damage to your stunning face, and secondly, his love for the stock trading and what he has achieved so far. I have decided to invest £30,000 with him on his terms. Rose, he will regain his manly functions only after six months. So, with patience and total family support, he will be nearly just as he was. Rose, your confidence and the twins will make all the difference; do not lose heart, even for a moment. He needs to see your beaming smile all the time."

Amma left the room and brought the twins, and the specialist was happy to see the babies. He gave them £10 to each child and blessed them. Rose thanked him and left to join James. Amma briefed others in front of James about what the specialist said, including his investment with James and the three were happy. Amma then took them out on the pretext of coffee and left the two some privacy. They kissed passionately after drawing the curtains and both were in tears. Later, they managed to compose themselves.

"Rose," he said, "I need my books to start trading tomorrow to prove that nothing affected my stock trading skills."

"I will bring them tomorrow and sort out a sliding table for you to look at the typewriter. I might even get it done now."

She got the maid to help the nurse bring a foldable overbed table to take the typewriter and notebook. Within an hour, all was ready, and James logged on. He remembered most of the details by heart and started investing, following his usual pattern. He was able to check the share values frequently. They went home for lunch and had a siesta. They came back at 4 pm and spent till 7 pm and left. They found James in excellent spirits. He made a 1/2 % gain on that day. Amma and Rose were happy, and so was the specialist. Rose set up an account in BSL with James to trade and for the consultant to check, who transferred £30,000 immediately.

A week went by and they removed the thick, tight belt. James could rest on his sides, which he avoided for a few more days to help with the speedy recovery. He diverted his mind with the stock trading, and he was very positive, highly encouraging, and showed a tremendous sense of humor to the nurses and other staff. Amma, Rose and visitors were cheered up each day during their visits. A maid stayed with him in the adjacent room, providing a good daytime cover for the nurses. Another maid came to cover the night shift. The particular consultant saw his investment go up by 5% in two weeks and took good care of James, and it pleased Rose and Amma. However, he felt James needed to stay for two more weeks to walk using a frame.

James learned to walk within five days. He tried to walk with two sticks but he wobbled. The particular consultant recommended one more week of stay in the hospital for physiotherapy and training on walking using the walking sticks and James agreed. Amma arranged for a physiotherapist to come every day for three months to train James, indicating cost should not matter.

When James finally returned home, there was a big crowd of people to welcome him. He was using a walking frame rather than sticks. The reception committee's presence moved him and he could see the twins more closely now. He asked Margaret how the Bar-B-Q was coming along. She said that they both ditched the idea forever. All were shocked to see the burnt areas at the back of his head. However, a thin growth of hair started appearing to mask the baldness. He got a barber to come home and remove all his hair like the American film actor Yul Brynner, who shaved all his hair since the film King and I in 1951. Strangely, James looked very smart with no hair and all approved it. No one could relate his baldness to the accident a few weeks ago.

James was in a spacious bedroom with all facilities as in Rose's bedroom.

He also had a study with all the typewriter facilities, but he preferred to work in the main office room. By the previous week, Asha had delivered a baby boy, and all in the clan were happy. However, in his excitement, Dennis managed to slip on the bathroom floor and injured his head and back. They took him to the hospital immediately. The doctor recommended a week's stay for carrying out the various tests, mainly to check for a blood clot near the brain. The scan was clear, and Peggy and all families heaved a sigh of relief. However, he came home after ten days, and the doctor asked him to take complete rest for two more weeks. After that, he should visit the hospital twice a week for three months for physiotherapy treatment for his back.

James took a cue from this and fitted all bathrooms, including Amma and Appa's bathrooms, with anti-slip handles at strategic points, and ceased using bathtubs due to their slippery nature. Seeing this, John, Rajesh, Jeff, and Keith made similar improvements in their bathrooms to prevent falls. Soon, Susan delivered a baby girl, completing all the delivery schedules for all the families.

A few weeks passed, and they all met in Susan's house, where Mary and John took control. After lunch, they all sat in the lounge as usual and for a few minutes, Susan brought her daughter in and then left.

"I am glad all the babies, parents, and elders are reasonably healthy," said Dennis.

"Never test providence, Dennis," warned Peggy. "Let us be grateful to God that we are a happy clan in this lovely part of London."

"I agree with Peggy," said Amma. "Due to the grace of God, we have James back in nearly full strength. That accident has shaken us and we are too careful these days, taking no chances. We are glad his mental faculties were never affected by his accident and he is slowly recovering from all the physical damage."

"James, I have a special request to ask you," said Dennis. "I have two sons, who are more trained in farming than finance. Peggy is a typical housewife and relies on me for everything. So, my request to you was to take care of my assets if anything happened to me."

"Dennis, nothing is going to happen to you," replied James. "But I would advise a couple of things you need to do immediately. Firstly, please write a Lasting Power of Attorney for Property and Financial Affairs. Secondly, write a similar Lasting Power of Attorney for Health and Welfare. You can only appoint two as attorneys. I suggest one should be your wife and your two sons could sign one each. Registering with the government is crucial. Then the documents become effective. It would protect you in case of severe ailments like stroke, heart attack, etc.

"If anything serious happens, your property and assets belong to those you nominate in your Will. They would have to decide who to look after the property and finances. Initially, after you, all would go to Peggy and only after her, they would go equally to your sons. So, she has to decide about me and not you, Dennis."

"What precious advice to us for the immediate future," said Dennis. "I will attend to it tomorrow. I only hope Peggy and my sons will think like me on appointing you, James."

"Should that situation arise, we would have none other than James to help and support us," said Peggy.

"James, what you suggested to Dennis, applies to all of us," said Mary.

"We would also set up the two Lasting Powers of Attorney immediately," confirmed John.

Straight away, Amma, Appa, Tara, Rajesh, Jeff, Nancy, Keith and Joe all agreed to do the same.

"The beneficiaries of the Wills should not expect more than 1/2% to 1% of return per week on investment with me," James advised them.

"James, you have to get the documents done for us, and we will sign the papers when ready," said Amma. "Please put Rose and Philip as the two attorneys in both applications."

"But, mum," said Philip, "I'd like James instead of me as the attorney in both applications."

"Since you suggested it," she replied, "I request James to be the second attorney."

"I accept," he said.

"James, please put yourself as the primary and me as the secondary attorney in both applications," said Rose.

"I agree, Rose," he smiled.

They all left for their homes.

After two weeks, they all confirmed they had signed the documents. The lawyers had sent the documents for registration, and all should be effective in six weeks. All children were growing up, keeping the mums, dads and grans busy. The mums were meeting in the gardens for more fresh air and sunlight for the children. The twins were walking and even with two maids, Rose found managing them difficult. However, they were all bundles of joy for the grans.

To everyone's shock, Dennis suffered a stroke and spent ten days in the hospital. They discharged him but Peggy and the family felt he should have stayed in the hospital for a week more.

The consultant told the family that the physiotherapist visiting every three days should speed up the recovery. Dennis's left side was affected for three days only. Targeted exercises meant he could move his fingers, arms and legs much more than when he came to the hospital. Dennis slowly started walking using a walking frame. Three days before leaving the hospital, he used only one walking stick. The day before leaving, he was walking without any support. The consultant felt he was recovering fast and hence, he decided he could go home.

Dennis improved tremendously and Peggy and her family felt very relieved. Despite these improvements, Dennis realized that stroke is unique in that there was no specific exercise one could do to limit it coming back. The doctors perform bypass surgery; once new tubes are in, the heart is as good as new. For stroke, no one can replace the nerves to the brain! Dennis knew stroke could reoccur at any time. The only safe precaution was to stop falling and injuring the head, leading to clots in the brain. This sobering thought had its side effects in that he became preoccupied with falls. He resisted walking distances away from home; someone may recognize and seek help from home if he fell closer to his house.

Despite all the knowledge and realizations, Dennis slipped down the stairs in his house. Unfortunately, he forgot to hold the handles and hurt his head. Dennis did not think much of it but got persistent headaches and his GP admitted him to the hospital. On taking a brain scan, they detected a clot and sadly he passed away in three days, at home in the early morning while sleeping. Dennis's demise was the most tragic news that affected the clan and shook everyone. There was a big void in their group gathering that no one expected to happen so soon. Appa was the most senior, but he was never domineering. Keith, Jeff, John and Rajesh were relatively young to take charge as a senior. The task fell to Amma to manage the group from then on.

Amma felt more and more responsibilities would fall on James, but he said it would not affect him as he would only handle stock trading. However, any physical commitment would worry him as he could never accept those responsibilities.

A few months went by and the six children kept the parents and grans busy and happy. James could walk unaided and regained his manly faculties but used one stick when he doubted the ground terrain. Rose was delighted on three grounds: on James being able to walk unassisted; regaining his faculties; the children sleeping in their room, and he shared the bed with her after nearly six months. Rose made sure James was not allowed to run around with the twins in case he sprained his back. This inability was a case of sadness in their minds, but his brothers made sure they played with the twins and their children. Because they lived as a big clan, the children had company and were trained not to fight.

"I am happy things are falling into the right place for you and us," said Rose one night in their bedroom.

"In many senses, you are right," he replied. "But there is one aspect which, as a dad, I am sad about. I can't lift the children, throw them up in the air, run around with them, etc. But, on the other hand, I am glad our brothers and sisters are helping enormously."

"Let us enjoy what we have," she said. "I am glad your mental faculties were unaffected and some physical ones too!"

They slept soundly and the twins did not wake up for a feed in the night.

At one of those dinner meetings in Mary's house, Appa gorged himself with tasty burgers and chicken. Amma asked him to control himself as he was diabetic, overweight, lacking in exercise with heavy drinking and smoking. The GP had warned him that he was a prime candidate for heart problems with overeating. Appa laughed it off and ignored him as usual. Appa was very fond of gluttony, one of the deadly sins. That evening, he had a massive heart attack, and he was 'gone' even before the ambulance and paramedics came. They certified the cause of death as heart attack, so no post mortem was necessary. All the family members were shaken, despite having seen the writing on the wall for some time.

"James, we all rely on you to care for us," said Amma. "I will be an excellent support to you at all times."

"It is sad for you to lose a husband of over 35 years and for Philip, Rose and Jason to lose their dad," said James. "Financially, Philip, his wife, Paula and Rose are very secure. Jason is doing well in his articles and soon will be self-supporting. Because of exceptional income from the paintings, the girls have doubled Philip and Paula's salaries. I have asked them to use Jason on an ad hoc basis to write articles for various newspapers and magazines about their paintings and portraits. They have already paid him £250 for one such piece and a few more payments to follow when others in media publish his article. I will set him up with his own company. I'd like to talk to Jason later on about his company and try a few of my thoughts for its continued growth."

A little later, Jason and James went to talk in the nearest office.

"Jason, you should focus on writing articles of interest to your age group, overlooked mainly by adults; on children's stories, if you can invent any; any friend of yours who is good at drawing funny cartoons, caricatures, etc; frequently, send articles praising other journalists' contributions. Do these promptly and regularly," continued James. "The rewards will soon follow. If you get paid £250 for any of your contributions, including your friend's funny cartoons or sketches, pay him £100. Be generous. Try to visit motor or fashion shows and even if they do not expect it, send your contribution to them. The organizers will notice you eventually. Never be critical. Also, try to make sensible, cost-effective and crowd-attracting suggestions. Slowly these will bear fruit. Keep me updated frequently. Good luck."

"James, for you, the group demands are likely to increase," said Rose. "So I will help Jason when he needs it."

Amma arranged the funeral of Appa in the local church. The whole clan attended along with a very few of his old contacts. It was a solemn ceremony and Mary nicely organized the wake using an outside contractor. The send-off was very fitting for a man who enjoyed a good living, focussing on drinking, smoking and eating. Amma remarked that it was getting to be an ever-decreasing circle. Two out of twelve seniors were no more.

"It was a sad day," reflected James, "but we should all learn a valuable lesson. As a priority, all seniors should exercise, control their diet and reduce smoking and drinking. They all need to do a combined activity like Yoga, swimming, aerobics, jogging, etc. They all should have good health and keep fit for the sake of the youngsters in the group. A male and a female trainer would help from next month. I will review the progress. I will bear all the costs."

The seniors disagreed and wanted to share the expenses and Rose agreed to apportion the individual payments.

"Brilliant suggestion, James," said Amma, "to take care of the seniors and stop the decreasing of the circle. I am glad you think of us as a large combined family, caring for everyone in the group."

A few weeks went by and all the seniors were attending various exercise sessions under the guidance of the trainers and they felt better for it. Then, the maid announced that an elderly lady had come to see Clare. Rose met the lady who introduced herself as Ms Barbara Fisher. Rose took her to the living room where Amma, James, Margaret, Clare, Nancy and Mary were present. Rose introduced them and the maid brought tea and biscuits, which the lady welcomed.

"Please call me Barbara," she said. "My friend whose portrait you did and who paid £60,000, asked me to see you, Clare. I noticed that portrait and we in the museum were very impressed. I am representing them and they have asked me to put a business proposition to you."

"I am pleased to meet you, Barbara," smiled Clare, "and intrigued with your proposal. I will listen to my brother, James, and whatever he advises goes."

"Barbara, you have put a tantalizing comment," said James. "We need to know the details for us to decide. Rose is the CMO of the company owned by Margaret and Clare, and Amma, my mother-in-law, a descendent of Royalty from King Charles I, is an advisor."

Barbara stood up and bowed to Amma, which Amma acknowledged, and asked her never to do that again. Barbara smiled and set out her plan.

"I am in charge of a museum and my committee has authorized me to discuss the details of the business proposition. We like Clare's portrait as she focuses more clearly when multiple characters are involved. She is also very good with a single character. We heard from another lady whose portrait Margaret did and she was so impressed that she brought it to the museum and we all loved it. Sadly, our resident maestro painter is over 65 years and retiring in six months. He understood that the girls were very young but he offered to train them before leaving. We need both of them and both fit our purpose to a T. We want to project them as the principal painters and their income would go into several thousand a month. They would be involved in restoring great masters' paintings and the museum usually gets several million in the annual budget to do those jobs. They would have a high profile and media following. Restoring old masters requires a lot of preparatory work and the girls would have several assistants to prepare the paintings for them, ready for the girls to work on them. Does this sound appealing to all of you?"

"Barbara," replied James. "I'm glad you are keeping the partnership of Margaret and Clare intact. So, we thank the committee for offering both of them work at the museum."

Barbara telephoned the museum and talked to one senior member of the committee. After a few minutes, she confirmed that they were happy about the quick resolution of the issue.

"Would they have a separate accommodation as they have here?" asked James.

Barbara wanted to see the present accommodation and was very impressed with the facilities. She said they had a large detached bungalow to stay in. However, they would have to work in the museum, and the studios were well-equipped.

"How long do they have to decide, and do you provide a bonus for joining the museum?" he asked.

"We would provide £15,000 each on joining and you let us

know in a week. They could complete already existing assignments there. We would sort out any issues with their contractors," confirmed Barbara.

James thanked her and Barbara went to the girls' studios to observe and discuss further.

"What is your gut feeling, James?" asked Amma.

"I think they would never get such a golden opportunity to train under a maestro, to work and have private accommodation. We would miss them in the short run. We also do not have to worry about several logistical issues if they stay here."

"I agree with your logic, James," said Rose.

"I also agree with you, James. I hope they agree too," said Amma.

The two girls came back after an hour and were ecstatic at the offer to work for the most prominent national museum. They wanted to confirm acceptance in 48 hours to Barbara after visiting the museum and checking all the details. Nancy wanted the girls to stay there and not move out but could see the opportunity for them and reluctantly agreed. Jeff accepted James's decision and blessed them with a beautiful future ahead of them.

The next day, the girls went to the museum. They were captivated by the work facility, the spacious bungalow accommodation and support services. The museum was a 30-minute drive from there and the girls wanted weekly contact with James and dinner with the clan. All accepted those requests. The girls left with a heavy heart in a week. Barbara warmly welcomed James when he went with the girls. She told her committee and all the artists about James's background and his love for his wife, Rose, and how he sustained the accident trying to protect Rose. She also knew about his skill in trading and she wanted to invest some money with him. He just smiled and did not comment. He saw the girls' accommodation and was impressed with the enormous size of the rooms and facilities. The museum allocated an automatic Austin Maxi 5 door Estate with a driver, and the girls started taking driving lessons. They came to Amma's place in the chauffeur-driven Estate car the following Sunday and everyone was very impressed. They could see that the confidence levels of the two girls had increased immensely.

Barbara telephoned and wanted to see James in a few days and came at 10 am. She also decided to stay for lunch. After coffee, Barbara told James to invest her account for £30,000. Rose gave her the document for trading and conditions to become an investor. Barbara followed those procedures. James left Barbara to discuss with Amma, which she enjoyed and after lunch, she left for the museum.

After a week, with Rose's help, Barbara became an investor. It was a great satisfaction to her to invest with him and she tried to hug James. He had to remind her that his back was still suspect and even Rose had stopped hugging him. Barbara gave him a shoulder hug only. Amma complimented James on taking care of his sisters by helping the person responsible for them.

7

A sudden dilemma!

Amma received a telephone call from Judy, her best friend who was close to the present royalty. She had been in Australia for the last 15 years, as her husband was PA to the Ambassador and due to her husband's health issues, they were relocating to London and given a house in the St John's Wood area. He was obese, smoking and drinking, compounding his diabetic health problems. He was 45 years old and opted for retirement. They had two girls and a boy. They had relocated about two weeks earlier and found out she lived close to Amma's mansion. Amma asked Judy to come with the whole family around 10 am the next day and spend the day with her, including lunch and dinner, which Judy readily accepted.

The following day, they all arrived at 10 am and met in the lounge with coffee, tea and biscuits. Amma invited all the clan and it was a packed house. Judy introduced her family and Mary introduced all and explained Amma to all. James wanted to talk to Judy's children with Jason and left for the adjoining room.

"You three would not find anyone better than James to help you with your career; try to be frank with him," said Jason.

"Please tell me what you do now, what you want to do, and what your dreams are," asked James. "However wild it might appear now."

"I am a very average student," admitted Nicole, "and not keen to go to university for further studies. I am excellent in freehand caricature drawings and won awards in the school. I'd like to develop that skill and operate as a freelance."

"I failed in 'O' levels and hate studies," said Tracy. "I like to do painting and do portraits and got awards in schools and the local community. I only want to pursue that and be independent."

"I am top in school and very good at maths," said Duncan. "I want to go to university and eventually take a Masters in Mathematics."

"Nicole," responded James immediately, "you help Jason and start earning this week. Please talk to him and do what he wants. He was looking for someone with your skill to work with him. You all are family members from now. You both go to the next room and discuss and I will join you after I reply to the other two. Tracy, you have come to the ideal place and I will take you to your studio for painting.

"Duncan, I will ask Asha to talk to you as she was brilliant in mathematics and she would fix you up with a university place. Let us join the others, and please inform your mum what was agreed."

They re-joined the others and Judy and Jack were pleasantly surprised that James had securely sorted out the children's future in an hour. Nicole and Jason left to discuss her new role. James took Tracy to the studio and asked her to do any portrait of her choice.

"Nicole," he said. "I think you should operate as a separate company and invoice Jason for any work you do for him. It would help if you did freehand sketches on visiting a library, church, sports hall, gym, etc. Just leave the drawings with them. You might get invited to children's parties and asked to draw any child or mum; they would pay you well. Slowly your income will grow. I will help you start your company tomorrow; let us meet at 8 am. Keep all portraits in a folder as a marketing tool. Even at home, you do sketches of people, and they might pay! Accept whatever they pay and thank them. Whenever you visit churches, please give free portraits to the Priests and a few biblical pictures, which they might display to attract visitors to the congregation to know your skills and help you in your business.

"Tracy, I liked your portrait, and I will take you tomorrow to the best museum in London to meet your sisters, Margaret and Clare, as well as Barbara, their head."

James left her to join Jason and Nicole. Nicole was very excited and brimming with ideas.

"Duncan, Asha will talk to you later today to help you."

"James, can we talk privately, please?" asked Nicole.

James took her to the next room and closed the door.

"I am not ashamed to admit that I prefer relationships with women to men," she told him. "I admit I am a lesbian."

"I am glad you told me," said James, "and we'll keep it a secret. Does anyone in your family know?"

"No one has guessed as I do not even hold hands with Vanessa, she's my close family friend for over ten years now, but we both feel the same way."

"Is she good at art and craftwork?"

"Like me, she is into freelance cartoon drawings, and she is much better than me. She should be coming to see me tomorrow. I will brief her; please help us?"

"I will be very confidential," he promised and told of his experience with two gay friends when other students avoided them. "Let us join the others as if we are excited about your work. Don't tell them about Venessa today."

They joined the others, all discussing artwork.

It was time for lunch and Judy's children were on Cloud Nine. Amma advised Judy to let James handle all issues and not interfere.

After dinner, when they were ready to leave, Nicole tried to hug but Judy told them not to hug James because of his accident. All three were in tears and gave only shoulder hugs. Finally, they thanked him for a beautiful day and left.

"When Judy came this morning," said Amma, "she worried about her family and the children and did not know what to do. James, you sorted out her problems within an hour and brought smiles on the two girls' faces they had not seen for the last few years. You are like a messiah to them and God bless you. Judy and her husband were in tears to know you were adopted and how you did not want to marry Rose because of our high standing and your lineage! In her, you have a good contact for the future. She knows about your trading skills and will talk to you in days."

"The two girls are very talented," replied James, "and I have a feeling, Barbara, would snap up Tracy to help Margaret and Clare. Duncan has to wait a few years before starting to earn as a very good academic. Nicole will develop slowly and make a good name for herself and the family. Judy should contact Rose for investment. Judy and Jack should join us soon and be part of the clan from now on. We are back to 12 seniors now, Amma."

"She already wanted to join the clan," added Rose. "And after three months, she wanted to invite everyone for one Sunday lunch in her place. She was so happy with you, James. She feels greatly indebted to you."

The following day, they all came at 8 am, including Vanessa and Judy was happy to introduce her as a family friend. James told her that Nicole had mentioned Vanessa the previous day and found out they had similar skills. He would like to open a Limited Company, mainly managed by both. James opened a company for Nicole and Vanessa and completed all the formalities in an hour. The share capital of the company was £1,000. The company was registered in Judy's name, as Nicole and Venessa were under 18. Judy was the only Director as well. Mary was the company secretary, with Nicole and Vanessa as joint shareholders, with her mum. Nicole bought stationery materials for her freelance sketches. James suggested that Nicole and Vanessa stay in the detached bungalow where Margaret and Clare stayed so that he could help them daily by having them closer to him. Judy readily accepted and the girls were grateful to James for giving them privacy. When James was alone with the girls, he gave the same advice he gave to Margaret and Clare, to be extremely careful. They immediately agreed and thanked him. They both found the studio had all the materials they needed.

Judy wanted to invest £50,000 with James, and she followed the usual BSL procedures with Rose and opened an account.

Barbara came at 10 am to meet James and talk about her investment. He introduced her to Judy, and she took over the conversation. Barbara was impressed with Judy's Australian background. Judy also said she had closer contacts with the present Government and Royalty. A few days went by, and Tracy was made an assistant for Margaret and Clare, with a good salary, but she had to commute from home.

Judy and Jack were delighted. To celebrate, Jack was drinking, which Judy did not know. He collapsed. Ambulance staff took him to the hospital. His sugar levels were high and he had suffered a mild stroke. The specialist in the hospital recommended a dialysis treatment, every four hours for three days a week. The consultant recommended a hospital stay for six weeks minimum.

Judy and Amma went to the hospital and arranged a family room. Due to rushing about, Judy slipped and fell in the bathroom and twisted her ankle. She was in agony and Amma asked Judy to stay with her. Nicole and Vanessa had started their business and were pretty busy. Tracy had a lot of assignments and was unable to visit her dad. Duncan joined University College London, (UCL) and was living in the hostel. Jack was not keen on spending money for a nurse or a helper for six weeks. James agreed to stay in the hospital, giving Jack some company. Rose set up James's room with IBM Golfball typewriter facilities to trade. James asked Rose to get modifications done to Judy's bathrooms as had been done to other elders, including his. She agreed to do so.

The following day, James was in a wheelchair with the IBM typewriter and had started trading. Jack thanked James for taking care of his children, and he felt he was leaving them safe in his hands.

"I will take good care of them under your and Judy's guidance. Would you please tell me about your life in Oz from when you went, to keep us busy?"

"I was very excited when we reached Oz and proud of my job role, even though it was just a PA to the Ambassador. The atmosphere there was electric. The UK ambassador had higher esteem compared to ambassadors of other countries. Our family was well respected and treated. We had to attend too many parties and a lot of protocols to follow. We were in the Ambassador's residence, which had high security at all times, day and night. At the same time, we were separated by suitable partitions so that we never knew what was happening in their household, nor did they know about our household.

"We were able to see the government working at close quarters. It had a close relationship with the UK, Canada, a few European countries and America. However, the relationships with other countries were a low priority. The local aborigines were ill-treated, similar to the slaves and the blacks in the USA. It did allow Indians, due to their high education and quality of their work performance and a few Pakistanis in the country making up the low-wage workforce."

"How were women treated?" asked James.

"Similar to this country. They were paid low and only 50% of the wages for a similar job done by a male. These applied to the British women who had emigrated. Other white women were treated a notch lower than the British women. They ignored other nationality women by denying several privileges."

"How are LGBT treated?"

"They tolerated Lesbians," replied Jack, "but were against Gay men. Bi-sexual and Transgender were not recognized. There were no government laws to protect LGBT as in the UK."

"How about free education for the children in schools and colleges?"

"Up to 'A' levels, education was free, but one had to pay high fees for college education. Still, many Chinese, Japanese and

American students came to study as fees were lower than in their countries. After studies, they stayed on, but highly paid jobs went to Ozzie nationality students. My children went to an International School, where the standards were high and my girls struggled through. We were glad there were no yearly exams as in India! Duncan was studious and we were very proud of him. Judy and I thought that if we could marry the girls off quickly, our problems with their future might be over. Strangely, James, you seem to have a way of dealing with the youngsters."

"Their art skills will catapult the girls to a much higher plane than any of us could imagine. Generally, parents do not discuss with their children as a friend would, and usually, the parents try to put their foot down and raise the temperature of any discussion. I am glad you and Judy left them to my suggestions and they responded well. Their marriages could wait till they are ready. Jack, may I ask you a very personal query about your life in Oz?"

"No topic is taboo, and please ask away."

"You are still an attractive man. With many hours of late-night work with secretaries, were you ever enticed?"

"I misbehaved with my secretary, Ambassador's secretary and our typist. However, all the lady members left of their own volition. I also misbehaved with the new staff who joined. The Ambassador was no saint and after every party, we had to wait for him. He misbehaved and his wife had affairs too. Finally, they decided not to have any children, making life easier. Judy suspected something but never quizzed me till today. I feel guilty, but I enjoyed the affairs without feeling any guilt at those times."

"How do you feel now?"

"These are par for the course and occupational hazards with high-profile jobs. We met one family in the early part of our Oz life, Janice and Randolf. Janice and Judy rarely talked. I had a sexual relationship with Janice for several years until they returned to the UK. I later learned Judy had a similar relationship with Randolf. For years we had separate bedrooms, and Janice being barren did not give rise to any complications due to pregnancies. I suspected Randolf was the father of Duncan, which Judy tried to deny. I knew I did not sleep with her for years. We maintained a wall of silence. Randolf and I never spoke to each other from the beginning, and we never visited each other's house."

"What would have happened if Judy had objected at that time?"

"It might have ended in divorce as she had no family in the UK, no siblings, and with no job, she would have struggled with the three kids. But my health issues started to come to focus, mainly Diabetes, which I did not control; I never focused on my diet or exercise. I was admitted to the hospital five years ago. It completely shook us, and then I started thinking of retiring. Diabetes affected my Erectile Dysfunction (ED), leading to depression. Judy told me not to worry about it as we already had three good children. She said women of similar age disliked sexual contact and it should not affect our happy life. So, I have not had sex with my wife for over ten years. We have learned to live with that."

"Jack, instead of thinking about what you were, please start thinking about what you are now. Please focus on writing a book to help the recruits entering the service. Teach them what to do and avoid relationships at work lest marriages end in divorce. You may also advise them to treat women with respect, not sex objects, and that one has to score. Do you like writing?"

"No, but I have a lot to say and would not mind if you would write as I dictate."

"I know a confidential writer," said James, "and he would take a few points and develop from them. You do not have to say everything. I could ask him to come tomorrow and start this assignment. In five weeks, you could see how the book would turn out to be. If you are keen, Jack, I could ask him to come tomorrow for discussion by 10 am."

"**Y**ou've changed my outlook, and I no longer feel I am a patient in the hospital with so many issues. I have a lot to think about and feel very positive about life. So please ask him to come tomorrow."

"I will pay the writer this time, and when the book is a sell-out, you pay me back and pay for future ventures. Mr Glen Murphy, 25 years old, bachelor, good-looking, modest and very secretive. He is very focused, does not spend time in idle chats and would get on with his work. One of my investors requested me to help him get some paid work. I will phone him now to come here tomorrow. You might tell the family you were writing about your experience in Oz and for the family to remember you by, in future years."

James telephoned Glenn. He was keen to come immediately to see Mr Jack on that day to start work and agree times to suit him. Unfortunately, Amma, Judy, Nicole and Tracy were in the hospital a few minutes before Glenn arrived. James took Glenn to Jack, who introduced his family to him. Jack told his family the reason for Glenn's visit to write a book for him. They all were amazed to see such a handsome man and Tracy was gob-smacked on seeing Glenn, and he was also impressed seeing Tracy. After all the pleasantries, the family left with Amma in an hour.

"Jack needs to have dialysis treatment four times a day, starting at 10 am, 2 pm, 6 pm, and 10 pm," said James. "He will have treatment for three days a week. He would also be tired after the treatment and might go to sleep. You might have to take notes when Jack is awake and develop those notes as you can. Jack was likely to be in the hospital for another ten to twelve weeks. He does not have any dialysis treatments during the weekends. I would recommend Glenn to come Saturdays and Sundays and miss weekdays except for Wednesdays. Let us review at weekly intervals and make changes as you both agree. Jack might use a dictaphone to record his thoughts for you to listen to the tape and write the story."

"That sounds fine to me," agreed Jack, "and I would also use the dictaphone, as you suggested, James."

"Glenn, I will pay £300 per month, and we expect a super life story from you in time," said James.

"James, I am so indebted to Mr Jack and you for this godsent opportunity, and I will not disappoint either of you. You are paying me well and thank you. I know shorthand and take notes quickly. Also, if anyone stole my stenographer's notebook, they need to know shorthand to read it!"

James went to the next room to let Jack and Glenn talk about the book. After an hour, Glenn came to the next room to join James and said he had enough material to start the prologue.

"Glenn, would you like a typewriter to type here or prefer to type at home?"

"I prefer to type here, but I have a heavy old model typewriter, which is not portable. Is it possible to use a modern typewriter here?"

"You can use this room exclusively for typing, and the nurse-carer would get us coffee/tea/snacks at 10 am and 3 pm and bring lunch and dinner at their mealtimes. Tomorrow, you will have a separate typewriter as it is nearly 5 pm now. I suggest you work from 9 am to 5 pm on the days you already agreed to work, and all is flexible as long as Jack agrees as well."

Glenn said goodbye to Jack and James for the day and when James paid him £100 as an advance, he was delighted. An hour later, the person who recommended Glenn thanked James profusely, stating he never expected a response so soon! James told him about how competent Glenn seemed to be and that maybe in a few days, they would be able to comment on his writing skills.

Since James shared the hospital flat with Jack, James was missed more on Saturday and Sunday clan gatherings. All made an excuse to meet in the hospital for a few minutes with James. All the five girls, Margaret, Clare, Nicole, Tracy and Vanessa came to the hospital and were awe-struck seeing Glenn. Tracy snatched a few moments to talk to him and found him shy and reticent. After a short time, he opened up, and she noticed he had a good sense of humor and was very polite to the opposite sex. They exchanged telephone numbers so that they could talk in the evenings.

Jack noticed Tracy and Glenn being together more and remarked to James that they would make a sweet couple. James told him to give them time to settle in their jobs, stabilize their earnings, and only after that focus on romantic ideas. Jack told James he knew how to guide the young people to take the right path, and it was James's responsibility.

"Now you have a ghost-writer to tell all your story," said James. "So, there is no need for our discussions that we used to enjoy before Glenn came into the picture."

"Too true, and I enjoyed our talk more. But this interaction with Glenn has focused on getting the book published soon. I find you are managing to get 1/2% to 1% weekly growth, and it seems you were not disturbed by our talks."

"I constantly watch the price movements, and if it is going down, I sell due to setting up instructions for sale. If the price goes up, I do nothing till 4.15 pm and sell all stocks after telephoning the BSL. I was never distracted. If I felt it affected me, I would have stopped chatting to find out what was happening. Trading is like my lifeline and for the clan and I have kept so far above my promised target. Since you would be busy with Glen five days a week, might I come only on those two days, Tuesdays and Thursdays, please?"

"I was worried when you would raise this. It is only fair to ask you to come just for those two days, however, I miss your presence here. James, I appreciated you being with me for the last three weeks."

After dinner, when Jack went for dialysis, James went home with the chauffeur, but a maid came to stay at night in case of assistance to Jack. Amma and Rose were happy that he was back home, and he was glad to be with the twins. After three weeks, Judy had recovered, and she and Tracy moved back to her house. Judy agreed to cover for James, for the two days instead of him and thanked him for the timely help. However, she could see some hesitancy in James and wanted to know why.

"I am having second thoughts about Glenn," he said. "He seems to be very courteous and well-mannered, but these could be deceptive. With five young girls in our group, he could present a problem."

"What are you going to do about it?" asked Amma.

"I need your advice about which way to proceed," he replied. "Firstly, I could stop him from working any further after reading the first draft tomorrow and eliminate the problem of his meeting the girls. But unfortunately, Tracy is fond of him and has his telephone number and has called him in the evenings. As a young girl, she would not think kindly to any of my doubts, and it is in this aspect I need your help. Secondly, say nothing about the 1st draft and strike when he misbehaves, which I think would be a bit late, and he might become a nuisance with other girls."

"Both are very delicate, but the first option is more manageable. I would take care of Tracy in the presence of her mum, Judy, who thinks highly of you. Then, you proceed with saving the females of the clan from young gropers!"

"James, I am impressed with your assessment of people," said Judy, "which has been spot on from what I have heard from others. I will try to help, following Amma's advice."

"Tomorrow, I will see Jack," said James, "as Glenn is bringing the draft to read. So, you do not have to go to the hospital. I would return by 4 pm."

James was in the hospital by 7 am to start trading early the following day. He briefed Jack about his concerns and discussions with Amma and Judy. Jack was in total agreement. James said he had another female ghost-writer, Ms Ethel, in her mid-30s, divorced with one daughter eight years old, Tara, and she was in a destitute situation. He hoped the work would progress very well, and he need not worry about revealing any gender issues. She would write what she heard. She had written for a male author about his seedy past bordering on pornography, and it had sold well. Jack was happy and keen to get rid of Glenn. James did not mention Tracy or her telephone calls to Glenn.

The following day, Glenn came to the hospital at 9 am and showed the draft to James. It read well but had two flaws. First, the language and the style were different to a person of Jack's age and experience. Also, there were many grammatical mistakes, which needed scrutiny. He talked to Jack, who read the draft but realized the shortcomings only after James pointed them out.

"Glenn, thanks for the short draft, but we have two reservations," and he explained them.

Glenn found it difficult to disagree with the criticisms. James advised him to write to match with the age and experience of the author. Glenn was ashamed about the grammatical mistakes and James advised him to get a tutor to learn more about grammar and its usage. Glenn agreed that he was not ready to be a fully-fledged ghost-writer yet, maybe in one to two years. He wanted to refund the £100, but James asked him to keep it and pay a good tutor.

"I understand you exchanged telephone numbers with Tracy, who thought you would be working for her dad. Now the situation has changed and please do not call her in the future. It is a polite request and even if she calls you, turn it down and please get a new telephone number asap. When you are suitably trained and passed an exam, please let me know to help you with any business available at that time."

"I promise not to call her or take her calls. As you suggested, I would change my telephone number. She made one call last night, and we spoke for just two minutes. I will forget I met her. I'd like to keep in touch with you."

"Please give me your new number, and I have your old

number. We wish you a focused study period," said James.

Glenn left after bidding goodbye to James and Jack. Jack admired James for stopping him from calling Tracy and as a sweetener to get him business once he passed his exams - a clever ploy to ensure he did not lie about calls to Tracy.

Then Jack remembered something important, an extremely delicate matter and needed to talk to James before calling Ethel.

"Many years ago, I had an affair with a young woman called Ethel. Judy and the family did not know about it. After going to Oz, I continued the liaison to visit London. She knew I was married, and divorce was out of the question as I told her that my wife was a devout Catholic, which was a blatant lie; Judy was a non-practising Anglican. It stopped Ethel from talking further about divorce. We agreed to split, but she was pregnant, and for the sake of the baby, we did a civil wedding to give the baby a legitimate dad. After a few months, we divorced, and from that time, my travel to London was hardly once a year. I completely forgot about her. Your mention of the writer, Ethel, and a baby daughter reminded me of her. I had completely forgotten about them all these years. I felt I should tell you."

"I haven't seen her or contacted her about writing for you. Shall I forget her and get someone else?" asked James.

"I'd like to meet her and the child I fathered. I left her destitute by paying £1,000 before I left her. I want to bear the child's education expenses and please James, take good care of her as my other children. I am not sure what Judy and family and the rest of the clan would think of me, other than being a scoundrel, but their opinions do not bother me."

"Let me suggest a different way. I will let you know tomorrow the best route to take."

8
An experience to forget

The following day, Jack was happy about meeting Ethel and her daughter Tara. He imagined how an eight-year-old daughter would react to seeing her dad for the first time. James promised to get a photograph.

Jack was reminiscing about the wonderful times he had with Ethel without the knowledge of Judy for several years when they were in Oz, and he used to visit London frequently. He never felt he was cheating on his wife. Jack was the master, the only wage earner, and that arrogance made him ignore the duties of a family man. He was more self-centred and oblivious of Judy's feelings, and in many ways, he had alienated her over the years. He was aware of that, but he ignored those feelings.

About 24 hours later, the maid said there was an urgent call from the hospital consultant. He wanted James and Judy to come to the hospital immediately as Jack had been in a coma in ICU for over 12 hours. When asked for details, he refused to give them and told Judy not to mention this to anyone or bring the children. James was as puzzled as she was and they went straight to the hospital.

The consultant took them to his office and told his secretary not to disturb him during the meeting.

"I am sorry to inform you, Mrs Dench, that your husband Jack has been in ICU since last night at 7 pm. He seemed to be happy after talking to James the previous evening. Against all written rules and instructions, one of the nurse's male assistants, a new trainee who joined six weeks ago, became friendly with Jack and bought him half a bottle of Scotch Whisky without telling his superiors. He left his shift in the evening but did not record the purchase and delivery of the whisky. We were alerted to go to ICU in the evening and the doctor showed us the empty bottle, which Jack must have consumed in a short time. Due to a sudden spike in his sugar level, he went into a coma and dialysis treatment became pointless. His condition changed from critical to terminal stage implying, he could pass away at any moment. That was when we called you to come to the hospital. If you had come earlier you would not have been able to see him as he was in ICU, and due to the risk of infection, no one was allowed to be inside ICU. My advice to you now is to go back home and wait for the hospital to inform you of the nearest funeral home."

"I am stunned to hear Jack is no more and the children will be so upset," said Judy, looking shocked.

"Last evening," continued the Consultant, "he seemed normal, cracking jokes with the nurses and staff. He called five medical people and insisted on adding a codicil to his will. It included me, two nurses and two junior doctors. All the five witnesses signed the four originals; these copies were sent to his lawyer by a special courier. He was sober and in a good mood at 6 pm. Within an hour, his condition became critical, and at 7 pm he went to the ICU. We were all shocked, and slowly we realized that he was drinking. After this time, you could not have stopped him."

"Why do we have to wait for the hospital about the funeral home?" asked James. "Could Judy and I see the body tomorrow?"

"It is not possible to see the body at any time," replied the Consultant "Jack told us that he had got a donor card for giving away his organs on death. This stipulation means the hospital doctor must remove the eyes, liver, heart, skin, etc., within a few hours of dying, and would mean the face without eyes. They usually wrap the body in sheets and a coffin with a sealed lid. The mortuary doctor told me that they would send, to the nearest funeral home, and you would have to contact them for the type of service you require. He told us he had opted for cremation and not burial."

"He did mention that," said Judy, "and we would stick to direct cremation, as in this case, the body in the sealed coffin would be going to the funeral home. I will arrange it with the funeral home."

When James and Judy returned home, she asked him to give everyone the sad news, then went to her room in tears and did not want anyone to see her.

James told Amma, Rose, Mary, and Nicole what had happened.

"What a shock to Judy and the children not seeing their dad in his last days," cried Amma. "A sealed coffin is not a great comfort. Maybe they should take an enlarged photo of him in his best suit?"

Nicole went up to see her mum, who was composed by then. She came down, and the others all hugged her. Nicole said she had to attend to her work in a few minutes.

"I am sad in one way," said Judy, "not to see him but glad that the bastard was thinking of his affair and drinking when he was forbidden. I want to know it all. James? You seem to know the details."

James reported back how he was talking to Jack, who frankly revealed all, particularly about the affairs with Ethel during the early years and about their daughter Tara, now eight years old, who he had not seen since her birth.

He was excited to see both of them and that happiness made him drink. He gave all the details, which infuriated Judy and Nicole, who shouted that one could never trust men. Suddenly, she realized her error and apologized to James repeatedly. Amma admired Rose for being blessed with the best man as her husband, and he took good care of the whole group, particularly all the youngsters' futures. All the elders agreed and James responded by saying he had the best woman as his wife.

The maid came in to announce an urgent telephone call for Mrs Judy or James. Judy took the telephone call in the living room and said that the hospital mortuary doctor was sending the body to the nearest funeral home about two miles from the Anglican church, which was a mile away. The funeral home wanted everyone to come by 2 pm on Thursday so that the minimal service could begin by 2.30 pm and finish 30 minutes later.

Rose informed the clan about the serious diabetes complications, which led to Jack's death the previous day; the funeral was on Thursday and all should meet at 2 pm, giving them the funeral home details. The family lawyer telephoned and expressed his condolences to Judy. For the reading of Jack's Will, he wanted the family to come to his office on Friday at 10 am. James asked the lawyer to come to the house instead, as it would be more convenient to get everyone ready in the morning after such a traumatic experience the day before. The lawyer agreed.

About thirty people attended the funeral, and it was a solemn occasion. A young mother and her daughter of 8 years came, and James arranged with the driver to take Tara home to see the twins and play with them. After some hesitancy, she went with the driver. They all thought she was a distant relation. Rose arranged food for the wake by a well-known local caterer, and the whole visit finished by 5.30 pm. The children were disappointed not to see the body. That evening all people in the house were prisoners of their thoughts, and no conversation took place. The only noise in the house was the twins' laughter, and they clung to Tara. Amma, Rose and Judy were very impressed with Tara. They all retired to bed early due to the busy morning the following day.

James dropped Ethel and Tara back at their house. On the way, Tara dozed off. Ethel wanted to know what to do as the only job as a writer was no longer possible due to Jack's sudden death. She was at breaking point. James said he had a secure job for her but would discuss it later. He assured her that she need not worry about her work, finance, or personal issues due to men demanding favors. Ethel smiled and thanked him. James dropped her and said the driver would pick both of them up in the morning by 9 am.

When he returned home, he found Amma, Rose and Judy there. All the others had gone home or to their bedrooms. James wanted to say something confidentially as the children need not know immediately. Judy was puzzled and wanted to know all the details. James told about Ethel and their love affair for many years till she bore Tara. Jack had never seen Tara, but he did a civil wedding with Ethel to give Tara a dad's name for the birth certificate. They divorced soon, and Jack never saw them. He was excited to know about Ethel as a writer for his experiences in Oz. He wanted to meet her the following day. Unfortunately, he was in the ICU at night, and there was no possibility of seeing her. His sudden death complicated the issue, and James told Ethel about the funeral home and advised her about attending. James asked her to be present for the reading of the will the following morning. Jack had asked James to look after Tara's living and education expenses, including the university, and James felt Ethel's presence was crucial.

"What a fine mess you got me into, James! How do I deal with her?"

"Now you know about her," he said, "and she knows about you. Let them see her as known to Jack, and your children will come to know more during the Will reading. She had the right to see Jack, but circumstances prevented that from happening. It was difficult to ask her not to attend the cremation ceremony. It is difficult to delay any further."

She reluctantly agreed.

"I am amazed James," said Amma. "You know so many details but reveal only a lit bit at a time. In this instance, the poor Ethel needed to see the family of Jack and come to terms with her life."

Judy's family of four, together with James, Amma, Rose and Ethel, attended the Will reading. The lawyer said that Jack had given specific instructions for the disposal of his assets, but he did not own any property at the time of his death. He also wrote a supplement in front of five witnesses a day before his death. The details, said the lawyer, were as follows:

"A. His total assets were UK £800,000, about £600,000, arising from the sale of his property in Oz.

B. He wanted each of his children to receive UK £15,000 on his death.

C. Judy should receive UK £705,000.

D. Tara was to receive UK £50,000 for her living and education expenses and James was to set up a trust fund for that purpose."

He then asked if there were any queries.

Ethel stood up.

"I want to return the £50,000 to Judy. How do we do that? James, would you please help me to return the money?"

"You and James have no right to give Tara's money away," replied the lawyer, "and she is too young to give her consent."

"Was there a short period for people returning to the UK to buy a property to escape inheritance tax?" asked James. "But now Judy has to pay

£240,000 - 40% on £600,000 - because he did not buy a property. It seems unfair to expect a returning family to purchase property in three to four months?"

"An excellent point," said the lawyer. "Let me clarify something from my office."

He telephoned his office and after a short period, he said with a smile that James had just saved Judy 40% tax. However, she should buy a property within eight months.

Judy was so happy, she went and hugged James, who stressed shoulder hugs only, which she did.

"James," she said, "please help me buy a big property in this area asap."

James telephoned an estate agent and asked him about a large property in the same area he lived in, with a maximum price of £600,000. He then asked the agent to speak to Judy about the house. After fifteen minutes, she finished the call and was happy about the swift movements on a house purchase. The lawyer took leave and asked James to update on the house purchase.

"It is nice of you to think about returning the money, Ethel but you have to bring up Tara, and you will need it," said Judy.

"And I would like you to stay with us in this house with no rent to pay," offered Amma. "Tara was so good with the twins and would bring a lot of help to Rose."

"I need to talk to you about a job," said James. "As your prospective employer is no more! Please tell me, what are your skills?"

"Apart from typing, shorthand and general secretarial work, I have no other skills apart from my writing."

"I would like you to assist two young artists who have their studios in the detached property about a five-minute walk from here," said James. "You'll have a salary of £200 monthly and nothing to pay for rent nor all your living expenses. The new Trust fund will cover Tara's expenses, including education costs. The two young bosses are girls and you will have no gender worries. This job is for life, and if you seek other pastures, I wish you good luck in your future."

"James, like an angel, you have given me a good salary with benefits. I will cling close to you and never leave you. You are like an adopted brother to me," said Ethel.

Amma asked the maid to show Ethel and Tara the bedrooms and other rooms for them. Ethel was stunned by the size of each room in her self-contained section, with a large bedroom and ensuite bathroom and a separate WC, walk-in closets, two rooms as offices and a separate playroom for Tara. Tara had a large bed and the twins started sleeping with her. The maid put the twins in their beds later in the night to sleep in Rose's bedroom.

The following morning the estate agent came and apologized for the sudden visit. There was a big five-bedroom property that had been put on the market last evening for £590,000 and it was a ten-minute walk from here.

"You can see the property in the next hour," he said. "The American family want to return to Virginia in two months and need a quick cash sale. Mrs Judy has no chain and I recommend you close the deal this morning."

Amma asked for the lady's name and said she had visited her in the past and that the house was big and modern. Judy went with Nicole as James had gone out, and they returned within an hour. They both loved the house and its proximity to the twin's place. James came back and after discussing with him, Judy made an offer for £575,000. The agent contacted the sellers and finally negotiated a price of £585,000 to which Judy agreed. She let James handle the finance. He, Judy, Rose and the twins met the sellers in the estate agent's office in an hour and exchanged bank details. Judy transferred the money to the agent the next day and the sellers were happy. They apologized for not seeing Amma and gave £100 for each of the twins.

"I never thought I would be the owner of a large property within a week of reading the will!" said Judy to Amma and James.

The lawyer was happy about the sale and assisted in transferring money to the estate agent. The house was huge and Nicole was ecstatic about their rooms.

"I am so happy," she said, "and Ethel you could move with us!"

"I am happy to stay with Rose," she replied, "and Tara would love to be in the same house as the twins. I thank you, Judy, for the offer."

A few weeks went by, and one morning, the maid announced a lady had come to see Mr Jack. Amma, Rose, Judy and James were in the lounge as she was brought in. James asked her to follow him and took her to the conference room. He told her that Jack was no more and his funeral was about a week ago. She nearly broke down and James tried to comfort her by hugging her. She told him that Jack was the man she had loved for several years. They'd had intimate relations as she did not get on well with her husband.

"What is your name?" he asked.

The lady said she was Janice, and he could call her by her name. She and her husband Randolf were in Oz for a few years, where they met Jack and his wife. However, they never met them socially or visited each other's houses.

"Janice, you do not talk of Judy, only Jack. Why?"

"I admit I had a sexual relationship for many years with Jack as Randolf did with Judy. Each of us knew about the other's relationships, and we turned a blind eye. I believe Duncan was the child of Randolf and Judy. After eight years of relationship, we returned to the UK. We learned Jack came back to London a few months ago, and I wanted to see him. Sadly, it was not to be. I'd like to return home. Please tell them I had to leave urgently. Thank you, James, for your patience in listening without making any judgment."

She left hurriedly and James came back to the lounge. He only said she had to return urgently to her flat.

"Did she say anything else?" asked Judy.

"She was very frank, linking both families. I do not think others need to know as the details were too personal."

Just then, the maid came to announce that a gentleman was asking for Mrs Judy.

"Judy, please take him to the conference room for privacy," said Amma.

Judy left and saw Randolf in the conference room. Before the maid could close the door, he pulled Judy to him and kissed her on the mouth, and she also responded passionately. After a few minutes, they separated and drew normal breaths. She told him that Jack died a few days ago and his funeral was about a week ago. Being very impulsive, he did not care about Jack's death and dragged her to the lounge and said he wanted to see his son, Duncan. It was a shock and news to all. Fortunately, there were no children to hear his outburst. James told Judy they should go to the next room to reply to the gentleman. The three left the lounge, led by Judy.

"Please call me by my name, and now I can answer your queries," said James.

"Please call me Randolf. Where is Duncan?"

"He is studying at UCL and lives in a hostel. He comes on weekends only."

"Randolf, no one knew about our relationship," said Judy, "and you dropped a bombshell a few minutes ago. They all know Duncan's dad was Jack."

"You never slept with Jack for years, nor I with Janice. Why are you hiding it now?"

"Randolf, what are your plans now?" asked James.

"My company has asked me to relocate to Sydney with a bigger job, and Janice and I are leaving for Oz in three days. I want to see my son who, I've never seen. I haven't even seen Judy since her pregnancy. We might retire in Oz and not come to the UK for a long time."

"Randolf, my humble request to you is to let sleeping dogs lie," advised James. "The three children do not know of you and your relationship with Janice. Their mum and dad mean a lot to them and the parentage issue would make them disrespect their mum. You are going for good; why foul up their relationship before you leave? Judy is coming to terms with so many issues, please do not complicate the matter further. You both know the truth but keep it quiet for the sake of her happiness. I will update you on Duncan's progress from time to time."

"Thank you, James," she said. "I'd like to live in peace with the three children. Randolf is going to Oz for good, and we might not meet again. It is better to part on good terms than with an unresolved issue."

"James, you seem to be a fair-minded person taking care of the youngster's future," said Randolf. "I am leaving in three days and I want to transfer £50,000 for Duncan's educational expenses. Would you please set up a suitable Trust Fund for this amount?"

"As I said earlier," replied James. "I want to avoid linking you and Duncan. Please transfer the money to Judy, and she will pay it to the fund. I will give her bank details to you in a few minutes."

He contacted the secretary, who typed out the account details of Judy and gave it to Randolf. Judy wanted to give him something before he left, which was at her house so she was keen to take him there. James told her that when he goes to the lounge, they might ask several questions and what he should do? Judy told him to reveal all but ensure the children were not there. James thanked her. They left within a few minutes and she told the maid not to expect her for lunch or dinner. James came to the lounge and all wanted to know what had happened, but James said after lunch. After lunch, they met in the lounge,

"We were shocked when Janice came and did not ask for Judy, did not talk to her, but she asked only for Jack," said Amma. "Also, Randolf asked for Judy only, not for Jack, and claimed Duncan was his son."

"It transpires that Janice had a sexual relationship with Jack for over ten years, and in the same period, Judy had a sexual relationship with Randolf. Both the ladies never slept with their husbands for different reasons. As Janice was sterile, there were no complications with children with Jack. Judy had to be careful and meet Randolf when Nicole and Tracy were not in the house. Duncan is Randolf's son and all the four knew, but Judy denied it to prevent Duncan from hating her, as he has always believed Jack is his dad. Randolf has not seen Duncan so far, and he was keen to reveal the mystery. I had to step in and make him change his mind. He wanted to pay £50,000 for Duncan's educational expenses."

James updated the developments.

"All these are confidential and not to be shared with any clan member. Ethel, your relationship with Jack, the children would come to know due to seeing Tara, but my comments, about the four of them, should never be known to the children."

"James, you seem to do a delicate task, to maintain the peace for everyone in the clan, including the welfare of the youngsters," said Amma.

It was tea-time, and to the surprise of everyone, Judy returned home early.

"Randolf wanted to make arrangements with the bank for the money transfer," she said, "for Duncan's education and his gratitude to me for knowing him for several years. He will talk to James about investing £100,000 for me, for the welfare of the children, and £50,000 for setting up a Trust Fund for Duncan. We will not be seeing each other for a long time and we enjoyed being together for over three hours in my house. He sent all of you his best wishes. I had misbehaved for several years, as did Jack, and I do not regret it. Now I want to protect my family with three children. If I had a brother like James at that time, I would have behaved differently. But it is never too late to pray to God for forgiveness."

"It is very commendable of you, Judy, to admit the past guilt," said Amma, "and we will ensure no one outside the five of us knows about what you said. We also promise not to discuss it in future."

"I need to pick up something from home," said Ethel. "I'll be back in an hour."

"I will drive you to your place," offered James, "as it gives us a chance to discuss a few things."

Ethel left with James and Tara stayed to play with the twins.

"I am not sure whether to stay with Amma and be with Judy now," said Ethel to James in the car. "Is it better to give her more breathing space and time? It was nice of Judy to offer to stay together, but advise me, as my adopted brother, what to do?"

"What would you do if you were in her shoes?" he asked. "Ethel, please follow your instincts."

"James, you are brilliant. I would have suggested what Judy offered me. Now I will accept and live as a big family helping her."

She picked up the items she wanted from her flat, and they both returned for dinner. After dinner, they all wanted to return to their bedrooms to read and retire early. Amma came to Rose's bedroom to talk. James was in the study and he joined them.

"It has become a complicated life for Judy and her children," said Amma. "These secrets were liable to come out later in their lives and create more problems."

"You're right," said James, "but she might have more problems by revealing it now. I think Judy should stay with us, and Tracy stays in her house, as she has started working. She needs to have more independence and freedom of movement. Nicole and Duncan would meet more in Tracy's house than here, and it's a good thing for the three of them."

"It was a brilliant suggestion," agreed Rose, "and we will work on her. James, you need to give her a job to keep her mind occupied."

Amma endorsed that view and James agreed to sort it out in a day or two. Then they went to sleep.

James asked Judy about her skills when alone in the conference room the next day. She smiled apart from sex, very little else, as she had never worked in her life. She did not do even 'O' levels, and her good looks got Jack to marry her at a very young age. They went to Oz immediately after. James went to talk to the secretary for a few minutes in another office. He asked her whether she could use an assistant to train for 6 to 12 months on clerical duties, answering the phones, typing, filing and delivering mails. She was happy to take Judy as her assistant.

James came back to see Judy and said that she would be paid a notional £120 monthly for minimal clerical work to assist the secretary. He advised her to learn typing to get some speed and take lessons to pass O-level maths. She agreed, knowing full well both skills were not to her liking. She told James that she would try for three months and if it was a waste of everyone's time, she would decide to live on the interest from her investment of £100,000 given by Randolf.

"It would be correct to set up two trust funds for Nicole and Tracy of £50,000 for each," said James. "There is over £100,000 investment all ready for you, and the returns of 10% per annum would be more than what you will get paid now."

"James, I want to be a lady of leisure and not work. I agree with the two Trust Funds, and please set them up quickly. I am so grateful to have an adopted brother like you. I would be of help to Rose in taking care of the twins."

"Thank you, Judy," he said. "Be a lady of leisure from now on."

That night, when Amma came to Rose's bedroom, James was there.

"What is happening with Judy?" she asked.

James explained that she had decided to be a lady of leisure and then briefed them of developments. Rose was happy Judy would help with the twins giving her more free time. They felt she had enough money to live on interest-only and not work for anyone. Rose claimed that in her house, there were five women not working and one man, James, working, and she wanted them to take good care of him. Amma felt James was blessed to have all their attention. They retired to bed feeling happy at the turn of events.

9

It never rains but it pours!

Randolf and Janice left for Oz for good intending to spend their retirement years there with a lot of worldwide travel for good measure. In two ways, Judy was relieved: the children did not know about Randolf or Janice and Duncan's life would not be affected by his lineage. Judy told Ethel she would be indebted to her if she never mentioned Janice and Randolf and Ethel promised never to talk about it. Judy and Amma went out of the living room and with Rose upstairs with the twins and Tara, this left Ethel alone with James.

"We were upset to know that you did not have food on the plate for Tara on many days," he said. "How did you survive all those eight long years?"

"I was able to get a secretarial job with a small estate agency company. The boss was more interested in my body than the typing. So, I changed jobs, but all the bosses were sex crazy. I refused to go to bed with them and the bosses sacked me. It was a difficult period for me, and when Tara fell ill, I had to take time off. Many bosses used that as an excuse to bed me. After struggling for three years, I finally got a lucrative job in the physics department at UCL. After six months, the departmental head, Dr Ron Jones, could not keep his hands to himself. While I was typing, he would come from behind me and fondle my breasts. He was young, unmarried and good-looking, and I made a blunder of having a relationship with him. Later, he married one of his teaching staff, who knew of our affair. So, I got transferred to the student union office, and then I felt I was reasonably safe. But my income was low and it was a hand to mouth existence until your call came for the ghost-writing job. The rest, you know very well, James."

"I am sorry to hear about the problems you had and glad you will have no such issues from now on. You control your destiny and choose your partner, whenever or wherever you choose. In a way, you are the monarch of all you survey; your right, there would be none to dispute!"

"Brilliant, James, to compare me with Robinson Crusoe!" she laughed. "I am well guarded here, and without your approval, I would not be close with anyone. You are a good judge of character and will be my guiding light in this area."

Amma, Judy, and Rose entered the lounge with Tara and the twins. James took the three to the next room and they all played together.

Nearly two months passed and no new people came into their lives with worrying information. On the contrary, Ethel was a great help to the two young bosses, whose incomes increased by the week. Ethel's monthly income rose from £200 to £300. Slowly she started to understand the girls' business and after taking advice from James, became proactive in helping them with their business. She was always looking out for or creating opportunities for the girls. She quadrupled their income in two months and all appreciated her enthusiasm.

One Monday morning, around 10 am, the maid announced that there was a gentleman to see Ethel. Amma, James, Judy and Rose were with her in the living room and Amma suggested Ethel met the visitor in the conference room. Ethel wanted James to be with her and he agreed. When the maid brought the gentleman in, he introduced himself as Dr Ron Jones, Ethel's boss of many years ago. He had difficulty locating her but managed eventually.

"Ron," said Ethel, "please meet James, my adopted brother, mentor and advisor. It's a great surprise to see you. How is your wife and is she with you now, waiting outside the house?"

"She divorced me," he replied. "Then three months ago she married the Administration Manager at UCL. Is it possible to go to a coffee shop and discuss this in private?"

"I am pleased to meet you, Dr Jones. I will leave you and join others. This room is ideal for your private talk. I will ask the maid to serve coffee and biscuits immediately."

"James, please stay here," begged Ethel. "I have nothing to discuss with Ron. It would be better if Ron leaves after coffee, and we do not need to meet again. Ron, I am exceedingly happy here and my present work in helping the two young girl artists keeps me satisfied. Tara is very involved with the twins, and this place is nirvana for us."

"I would like to marry you, Ethel," he said suddenly. "Please take your time and let me know?"

"I am very flattered," she replied, "but I am not looking for marriage with anyone, either now or in five or even ten years. You were a womanizer and keen to bed them at every opportunity. I made a blunder of entering into a relationship with you, due to my need to support Tara. Now I am well-settled thanks to James and I work for myself invoicing the two young girls for my services. I am self-employed and take care of my pensions, tax, NI, etc. So, find someone else to marry, I never want to see you again, Ron, good day and goodbye!"

Ron obviously felt very disappointed and after coffee, he left but wished her all the best for the future. Then, she and James returned to the lounge. Ethel briefed the others on her conversations with Ron but said nothing about her past relationship.

After a few weeks, James had a telephone call from Barbara, requesting him to come to the museum alone for some private discussion. He was puzzled as indeed were Amma and Rose. He did meet her, as requested, at 10 am one morning, with lunch and afternoon tea also. After the formalities, Barbara opened the discussion.

"I do not want to shock you, James, but I've learned that Margaret and her friend Clare are in a Lesbian relationship, as the maid saw them in the same bed one morning. They had worked very late and were still asleep when the maid cleaned the room. She left the room before either woke up and saw her. However, they must have realized, as the maid left some cleaning gadgets in the room. It happened two days ago and I haven't mentioned it to them yet."

"It is better to have them here while discussing their relationship," said James. "They must be aware of your comments. You also know from the horse's mouth the background. It is better to meet on neutral ground, not in your office or studio but maybe in a hotel where we take a separate room for two hours and make it friendly and informal."

Barbara agreed and her assistant booked a hotel within two miles of the museum, for three hours for a private lunch. The assistant contacted Margaret and Clare and the four of them met at 11 am in the hotel. They ordered early lunch at 12.30 pm and had coffee before that.

"Barbara has told me how your work is progressing," said James. "It seems the maestro is immensely pleased that he was able to train two young artists. I'd like to have your comments before we move on."

"I can speak for both of us," replied Clare, "and we guessed why we are meeting suddenly here. We enjoy the work and feel privileged to train under such an eminent teacher. We wanted to raise a subject that had been troubling us for the last two days. We had strictly followed your instructions till that day. After a very late night, we forgot to put the 'do not disturb' card outside the door and did not wake up till 11 am the following morning. It appeared the maid had come to change the sheets and left hurriedly after seeing both of us on one bed. She hastily left a few gadgets, which we saw and realized our blunder. We guessed she would have reported to Barbara and, hence, this meeting. I will tell you our background, Barbara, which James knew from the beginning."

She told her the whole story.

"James," said Barbara. "I am surprised you knew all this and kept it a secret from me, knowing they would be working for the museum."

"You recruited them for their skills," he responded, "and not based on their moral issues. Even the law stipulates the employer has to recognize LGBT and not penalize employees."

"This is the first instant of LGBT I have experienced, and I need to consult with the museum committee. For the moment, please continue as if nothing happened, but if the committee disapproves, they might sack both of you."

"Barbara," warned James, "you are on shaky ground for three reasons: firstly, the current law forbids you to penalize any employees on the grounds of LGBT; secondly, you might act and influence the committee due to your prejudice; thirdly, you have already employed a person at a very senior level for over

30 years as a gay person, which you did not find out. These alone would result in the museum paying out huge compensation or you losing your job. So please, think carefully, Barbara."

"When and how did you know about the retiring expert, and why did you not let me know?"

"As Clare mentioned to you, two of my friends were gay, and only I was compassionate to them and learned a lot. When I met your expert, I noticed some traits, and while talking, he told me so many things. My unsolicited advice was to get on with other issues and ignore the lesbian aspect. I would ensure these two idiots do not make such blunders."

Reluctantly, Barbara agreed with him and they all had a quiet lunch, after which the girls went to their studio for a short chat with James. They thanked him for saving their skins!

"James," said Barbara, before they parted, "would you be prepared to work for half a day, each week as our consultant in the Personnel department?"

"I would work as an assistant to you, but not for the Personnel department," he replied. "Please give me a week to decide."

James came home and late that evening, he briefed Amma and Rose. Amma felt if he could spare the time, it would protect the girls. Rose suggested noon to 3 pm on Wednesdays so that his trading hours are safe. James offered Barbara the three hours on Wednesdays, and she was delighted. He went on the following Wednesday as Barbara wanted him for a committee meeting as a silent observer, and on that condition, they agreed to James attending.

At the meeting, he noticed that eight members were all over 60, except Barbara and the finance man who was in his mid-forties. He also observed how, apart from the accountant, everyone agreed with whatever Barbara said as the Secretary. The accountant, Steve Knight, was nit-picking, and James felt some of the comments disagreed with the notes handed out with figures. He made a note and listed the errors which Barbara noted. She defended her stand, highlighting the mistakes. When the committee voted at the accountant's request, he lost 7 to 1. He was red-faced and looked at James with anger but could not identify any accusations. He offered to resign due to other commitments, and the chairman accepted immediately.

The meeting was closed and the aggrieved accountant left. All the other committee members wanted to know how Barbara defended the accusations, and she showed the notes made by James. The committee was impressed and asked Barbara about James's skills. She gave an account of his trading skills. James excused himself due to another assignment and left. The chairman and others wanted James on the committee and asked Barbara to ensure he agreed. She said she was doubtful but would try. The chairman said James would have a remuneration of £3,000 per year even though all the committee members were voluntary. Barbara said James would not expect any payment and she would try.

When James returned home, he updated Amma and Rose as others were not home. They were very impressed and learned that the present accountant had resigned out of anger.

"What a fine mess I got them into during my first meeting!" he laughed.

Just then a phone call came in for James. Barbara had arrived and wanted to see him. He invited her into the lounge, and she was happy to see the twins and Rose and Amma.

"James, I want to let you know what the chairman and others

have asked me to do," she said.

She relayed all the details and said they wanted her to persuade him to be their accountant and that he would receive a notional amount yearly.

"It seems a very prestigious offer and responsibility," said Amma. "It must be very tempting, and I hope, James, you will accept it."

"I need to know the hours per week, the staff I have to oversee, and the responsibilities for seeking funding from outside sources," he replied. "I'd like to talk to all the people on the committee, individually and collectively."

"The museum operates differently," said Barbara. "All sections operate like a corporate organization. We, on the committee, represent each section and liaise with the top person for the department. None of us has direct administrative control over anyone. Your hours would be three on the day of the meeting and two on the day before to collect relevant facts for the meeting."

"Very well, I accept the role," said James. "Please convey it to the committee. I do not need any remuneration, as I would do it for free."

"James, we were all supposed to work for free. However, it was forced on us to accept a notional payment. So, please conform to the norms," said Barbara.

"I accept, Barbara."

Barbara telephoned her chairman and conveyed the good news. She then left for the museum.

A few weeks went by, and James was attending a monthly meeting of the committee, and after it ended, the telephone operator announced that a lady wanted to see Barbara. The lady in her late twenties entered the room. She was slim, blonde, and had style in the way she walked and talked. Barbara introduced James as her PA and asked the lady whether she minded him being present.

"Mrs Barbara, I am Michelle, and I do not mind James being present. I have heard favorable comments about him from my friend Judy, and I hope he will help me."

"Michelle, how may we help you?" he replied. "Also, your comments might involve the committee in deciding the best way to proceed. We may tape our conversations for them to hear and decide for themselves. Do you have any objections, please?"

"I have no objection to your taping the conversations. I used to work for the museum as a temporary typist in the Accounts section. I met Steve, and I fell for his good looks and charming talks. Within three months, we had a close relationship, and he indulged in a sexual relationship in his office during late nights on the pretext of typing urgent letters. I found out I was pregnant and told him. He said he was single and implied that he would marry me, but I found out later he was already married. I also found out he had made two previous temporary staff pregnant and paid for their abortions. I have not decided on the abortion route yet."

"James," said Barbara, clearly shocked. "Would you talk to Michelle, and I will listen?"

"Michelle," he said, "what is your objective for raising the complaint? There are several other queries for which one needs answers to get a comprehensive picture before the committee decides to act."

"Please let me know your queries," she replied.

"Was the relationship at any time forced or consensual? Do you have a record of all dates and times of the sexual activities in the office? Did he promise to marry you? Did you ask him whether he was married and what did he reply? Let us proceed following your replies to the above."

"Brilliant, James," said Barbara.

"I must admit it was consensual," replied Michelle. "I got worried once I fell pregnant. I have most of the dates and times we had a sexual relationship on the settee in the office. He said he was not married and never said anything about being married. My objective was to ensure he did not trap other temporary staff with close liaisons."

"Well," said James, "with your candid answers, you have shot yourself in the foot. The only avenue you left the committee is to discipline Steve for using the office premises for his sexual pursuits. He might not be allowed to seek further work for the committee, and neither would you. It would be hard for you to find a suitable job to support a young child. There is a way to resolve this, but you might disagree. Were you expecting financial support for the child by refusing to abort as per his suggestion?"

"I did not want to abort as it amounts to killing a life. I am aware of the complications in bringing up the child but only on moral grounds do I detest abortion."

"Were you a practising Catholic or less religiously inclined?" asked Barbara.

"I never had a strong belief in any religion, including being a Catholic. My parents, who live in Ireland, do not know of my pregnancy, and they would disown me either way! I have no siblings. They are poor even to support themselves. I send small amounts monthly, but as I do not have a job now, and might not be able to pay the rent and living costs from next month."

"The committee might decide to play it low key, talk to him privately, and warn of no future employment here," suggested James. "A similar situation would apply to you. This way, there is no control over his future misbehavior in other organizations. By appealing to help the lady in distress, mainly due to his involvement, he might pay a one-off payment for supporting you. Steve might pay or not, and the committee is not responsible."

"James, I agree with your comments. May I request help from you? Would you be able to get me a suitable job?"

"My advice is to wait until the committee decides and proceed slowly. When is the baby due?"

"In seven months."

"It means for the next 13 months, you might not be able to seek any work, and even after that, you would have to incur expensive child-minding costs," he said.

"I am broke now, and I did not want to sell my body to earn a living," she said bursting into tears.

Barbara hugged and consoled her. James gave her £250 for immediate expenses, non-returnable, the only condition. Barbara said the committee would meet today and after hearing the tape, decide on what action to take. Hopefully, they would see Steve in the next two days and know the outcome immediately.

"Michelle, we will inform you soon," she said. "Please give us your bank details for any money transfer to your account.

Michelle gave her bank details to Barbara and left after

thanking her and James.

"James, you were brilliant," said Barbara. "I admire the way you led her and made her admit her intentions. Let me get the committee in our office."

She asked the assistant to bring the other members in and requested them to listen to the tape, and she stressed the urgency of the situation. She left with James to the coffee room. The assistant called them to meet the others as they had listened to the tape twice!

"I must commend taping the conversations as it removed bias during verbal reporting of the details in the absence of the tape," said the Chairman.

"That was due to brilliant thinking by James," said Barbara.

"James," said the Chairman, "we agreed you have interviewed without any bias and in the best way for the committee. However, we all feel that you should talk to Steve on our behalf, and the committee would honor whatever you decide."

"I am very flattered to hear all your comments. I would need Barbara to be present in the talk, for two reasons. First, Steve had a poor opinion of me the day he resigned. With Barbara present, his anger would be less, and as the issue involves another female, her presence makes more sense."

They all voiced their agreement.

The assistant told Barbara that Steve could come for the urgent meeting in an hour. Barbara and James had a quick lunch and waited. When he arrived, after the pleasantries, Barbara got down to business.

"Steve, we have several grave issues, and the committee has

decided that James should conduct the interview."

"When I resigned a few days ago, I had only bitter feelings against James. Keith, a friend of my dad, spoke highly of him and he told me so much that my perception of James changed immediately. I am happy he is in the meeting and conducting the interview."

"I am touched by your comments, Steve," said James, "and I hope we leave the meeting with a similar good feeling. We had a visit from Michelle, and we taped our discussions. We would like you to listen to it, in private or with us. Which would you prefer?"

"Please turn the tape on and let us all hear," he replied.

After half an hour, Steve wanted a coffee break, and the assistant brought coffee for all. They drank it with chocolate biscuits.

"I can see that you have interviewed her, being fair to Michelle, the committee, and to me. I had not lied to her, which she had admitted. I came to know she was two months pregnant. Due to goodwill, I'd like to pay her £4,000 for her expenses for a year as she is destitute. I want assurance that she will not expect more payment after this."

"There are delicate issues for the museum," advised James, "which we could not put in writing. Firstly, we would want your verbal guarantee that you would not seek employment with us in the future. Secondly, we understand your wife is unaware of your relationship with Michelle and the baby. So, we would keep it that way. Finally, with a child to take care of and child-minder costs, the committee feels £7,000 towards expenses for 13 months would be more appropriate. Steve, we hope you agree to the payment amount. After Michelle receives the payment, none of these meetings would be on the museum's files, and the tape will be destroyed."

He then gave the bank details to Steve.

"Thank you, James, here's my check for £7,500, which she could credit to her account today. However, I do not want to see her but wish her well for the future."

Steve left immediately after thanking James and Barbara. She asked the rest of the committee to join them with Michelle in the staff canteen.

"In James," announced Barbara, "we have a mature negotiator. He let Steve listen to the tapes who then offered £4,000 for the expenses for a year to Michelle. James then very cleverly brought out four points."

She relayed these and said that James told it in such a way, Steve must have felt he was being extremely good to him. He managed to extract another £3,500. She gave the check to Michelle, who could not believe it, nor could the rest of the committee. Michelle rushed to kiss James, but he eased her aside.

"Michelle, you should resist this urge to show your affection; maybe this is what got you into trouble? Please go to your bank now, credit your account, and show us the receipt today so that the committee can destroy all records, tapes, etc."

Michelle went to the bank, returned within an hour and showed the transfer slip to all the committee members, who then agreed that James could destroy the tape. After a few pleasantries, they all left and felt satisfied that it had been a most successful day for all. Before leaving, Michelle gave her contact details to James, and he asked her to accompany him to see his family. Barbara knew Michelle's future was secure in his hands.

Back at the house, James introduced Michelle to Amma, Rose, his mum and dad, Ethel and Judy. Michelle was delighted to see the twins and the stunning beauty of Rose. James told Michelle that as the tape was in his possession, she asked Rose to play it to update others. James left them and went to play with the twins upstairs. The ladies listened to the tape, empathized with Michelle and praised James for getting more money. Michelle had a long private chat with Ethel, relating to her experiences.

"Michelle," asked Amma, "please tell us when the baby is due? When did you check with the doctor in the hospital? Did you feel the movement of the baby?"

"In seven months," she replied. "I had no tests or checks for two months, and I did not have money to pay for the doctor. I haven't noticed any movement yet."

"I'd prefer you see a Paediatrician and get an up-to-date test," said Amma. "You do not have to pay her, and she will come home later today. Not having a tummy for the first pregnancy is not unusual."

Rose telephoned her Paediatric Consultant, who agreed to visit in half an hour. They all had a quick snack with tea or coffee. James joined them for snacks as the twins were asleep after a hearty feed. Rose updated him and said they were expecting the consultant to check Michelle. The lady consultant arrived and first went upstairs to see the twins. After a few minutes, she came down and Amma introduced her to Michelle. The surgeon took her into the next room. She ascertained issues about pregnancy, did a few tests, said she needed to test her in the hospital, and asked to see her there in 30 minutes.

Michelle and others felt confused, but the consultant did not give them a chance to talk. James took Michelle to the hospital;

he assured her not to worry about anything until the results. The consultant took a few scans and more blood tests in the hospital. A midwife in the hospital also examined her. An hour later, she had most of the results.

"Michelle, do you mind if James is also present?" asked the Consultant.

"I consider him as an adopted brother, please let him come."

"Michelle, we have done the checks, tested your underbelly, taken the scans and blood tests. These indicate that you have APS, which can cause both low-grade symptoms and potentially fatal events due to blood clots. Some people are affected by symptoms more than others. Some have the antiphospholipid antibodies (aPL) in their blood but do not develop any blood clots, experience pregnancy complications, or display any symptoms at all. Doctors still do not know the cause or why these anomalies exist because so much research still needs to be carried out."

"What does it mean for my baby?" asked Michelle anxiously. "Is it alive, or am I going to have a miscarriage?"

"APS is usually associated with recurrent miscarriage, but it can also cause other pregnancy complications. The majority of miscarriages in women with APS occur at the early stages of pregnancy in the first 13 weeks. You are nine weeks pregnant and might experience complications from now. The typical low-grade symptoms of APS are headaches and migraines, memory problems, dizziness and balance difficulties, cognitive (thought) difficulties, joint pain and fatigue. Please contact your doctor immediately you experience any of these symptoms. Michelle, where do you live, and who is your GP?"

"I live in Hackney," she replied, "due to low rent flats. My

GP does not see many patients. I am worried about my safety there."

"You can stay with us from tonight," said James. "Let us go to your home and pack your clothes for your stay. We will discuss other details later."

"I am glad you will be staying with Rose and her family," said the Consultant. "I feel happier now. We have finished, and I will leave to attend to my other work at the hospital."

James took Michelle to her flat, which was in a dilapidated area with minimal facilities in the kitchen, only one bedroom, a small bathroom, and WC. It was damp and the wallpaper was torn and peeling off. James felt it was good she was moving out. They packed her clothes in one torn suitcase and other essentials in a few shopping bags.

On the way home, Michelle said,

"I regard you as an adopted brother, and I'm so glad we met. I am also grateful to you and Rose for allowing me to stay. However, I have a small doubt about the money paid by Steve. If I lose my child, and you get me a job, do you think I should return the money, at least a part of it?"

"Michelle, he does not need to know you are staying with us, and you will get a job through me. Let me talk to him on the telephone and take it from there. Your physical and mental pressures should account for something. He was a womanizer and filthy rich due to his wife, and he would not miss a penny of it. On second thoughts, we will do nothing."

They returned home for dinner and James updated them all.

"I am sorry to hear about the worrying diagnosis," said Amma.

"But for you, Amma, I would not have found out all these details. Thank you for alerting me to get things tested. Also, I thank you all for getting the consultant to do all the tests at no cost to me. As it is usually said, it never rains but it pours. My life has been a list of failures with no light at the end of the tunnel. I trust my adopted brother, James to help me lead a quiet and peaceful life.

10
Teach a man to fish, you feed him for a lifetime

Slowly, everyone was anxiously awaiting changes in Michelle. Rose arranged a nurse and a midwife for a few weeks to assist her. As predicted by the consultant, on the 13th week, Michelle suffered a miscarriage. The consultant, the nurse, and the midwife took Michelle through her painful and emotional journey. She was in bed for three days with a maid taking care of her. The consultant recommended some daily medication of low-dose aspirin to prevent miscarriages in the future.

By the fourth day, Michelle was back on her feet and comfortably getting on with her daily routine. James asked Barbara to come one morning, and he took her to the conference room. Michelle joined them in a few minutes. James updated her on all discussions with the Paediatric Consultant, and about not returning the money to Steve, even part of it. Barbara agreed as her motto was to let sleeping dogs lie. James left the room for a few minutes to allow Michelle to explain the miscarriage and associated issues. Barbara hugged Michelle, advising her to be brave and make the most out of the stay with Rose and her family. James asked Barbara not to say about Michelle being with Rose or her miscarriage. Barbara agreed and returned to the museum.

Two weeks passed with no issues relating to Michelle occurring. She recovered fully and wanted to find work. James asked her to rest for two more weeks before worrying about jobs. The maid came in to say that a gentleman had come to see him and she had asked him to wait in the conference room. James was surprised to see Steve. He greeted him and asked about any issue he wanted to discuss.

"I heard through my sources that Michelle had a miscarriage a few weeks ago."

"Have to come to express your sadness on the tragic way it turned out and why have you come to see me?"

"I wanted to convey to her personally how sad I was."

"Only a few weeks ago, you never wanted to see or hear from her, fearing she might ask for more money, and at that time, you did not seem to care about the baby. Now you seem to have changed?"

"I thought I should have some repayment of the amount I paid to her. With no baby to take care of due to miscarriage, Michelle's living expenses should be less, and it is only fair she gives back some of my money."

"I am astonished at your gall in expecting repayment," said James angrily. "Steve, please let me know how you got the information about her miscarriage? She could complain to the NHS about the lack of confidentiality. Once she makes a complaint, that person could lose their job. Is your repayment worth more than the job? Michelle had to go through physical and mental suffering almost every day and my psychologist friend felt Michelle should demand more money following the trauma, a further sum of £8,000 at least. She advised Michelle to bring a civil case against you, but I stopped her from taking that route. I told her to recover fully in two to three months, focus on the future and forget about you. She is reconciled to my advice. Steve, would you like Michelle to proceed with her complaint to the NHS? Or will you forget about your payment to Michelle from now on?"

"I am sorry for demanding repayment, and please forget we met today. You will never see me again," said Steve. "Good night!"

He left, and James shut the door behind him, murmuring, "Good riddance."

He joined the others and described the whole discussion he had just had with Steve. Michelle was so happy that she did not have to get rid of Steve. Amma praised James's machiavellian strategy of the psychologist and her financial assessment of the pains to Michelle.

This peace lasted for one week only. On Monday at 10 am, the maid announced a gentleman had arrived to see Mr James. Steve, who had promised never to see him again, had returned within two weeks! James took him to the conference room and asked the maid to bring tea and biscuits, which Steve welcomed. After that, Steve wanted to make a big complaint about the Museum committee personnel as they had not kept their word to him. James excused himself and called Barbara to hear Steve's complaint immediately. Steve agreed to wait until Barbara came.

"There was a verbal agreement that they would not reveal anything about Michelle, but my wife, Philippa, is on the warpath and instituted divorce proceedings against me. She seems to know all the details of our conversation."

"I apologize for what's happening, but I can assure you, Steve, that neither Barbara nor I am responsible for any leaks. I need a few hours to ascertain the source; could we meet at 2 pm, please?" asked James.

Reluctantly, Steve agreed and left. Barbara talked to each committee member, and they all denied any knowledge of the leak from them. James asked Barbara to find out whether any member was related to or close family friend of Philippa. Barbara started ringing again, and to her surprise, she found out that Phillippa's dad had been a close family friend of the chairman for over 30 years. Barbara asked the other committee members for a crucial meeting at 2 pm.

The maid came to say a lady called Philippa had arrived, wanting to talk to Mr James. She took her into the conference room, and James introduced himself and Barbara. Philippa was an attractive and stylish lady with blond hair and exuded sophistication. She declined their offer of tea or biscuits.

"I am the wife of Steve, who I understand has misbehaved again."

She talked about his womanizing tendencies, and this was the fourth time he had made a woman pregnant. This time the payment was more than for a simple abortion. She said that money did not worry her as much as his philandering, and she had instructed her lawyer to start the divorce proceedings.

"Ms Philippa," said James, "we are sorry to hear that, and before we reply, we need to know how you knew my address to come here and who told you about Steve's misbehavior and the money payments?"

"I am not at liberty to reveal the source."

James asked Philippa to follow him and asked Rose to meet her. She had her twins with her. On seeing her, the twins ran towards her, and each one held her hands. All were surprised as the twins never reacted like that. Philippa was so touched and said that you both must be lucky to have such beautiful twins.

She opened her handbag, gave each one £50, and handed it to Rose. Rose and James thanked her. Philippa asked James to call her by name in the future. They both joined Barbara in the conference room. The maid said the gentleman who came earlier had returned. She took him to the conference room as directed by Rose. Steve hesitated to enter but could not refuse to join the group. Philippa was initially embarrassed but reconciled due to unavoidable circumstances. Barbara, in the meantime, had asked the chairman to join the meeting, and he was also present.

"I have to wear my museum committee hat and speak on their behalf," said James. "Philippa, you made several statements without giving any facts and proof. We have to assume that you had concocted these without any factual evidence. For us to believe your comments made earlier, we need to know: who told you these, if these were facts, when did they tell you, when were these to have happened, who are the parties involved, how much was the money transfer, what proof, you have about the transfer, who are the parties involved in the transfer, who told you about my address to contact? It is unusual to have a very sophisticated lady like you dropping in and throwing several allegations at the museum committee. Therefore, I will ignore what you have said and claim that the committee has no basis to answer."

"I am surprised that you make me a liar throwing unfounded accusations," said Philippa. "It relates to my husband Steve's adultery with one of the museum staff and his paying her £7,500 relating to her pregnancy. I have seen the bank statements of his account indicating the debit to credit the lady in question, which details I do not have."

"Even though you have given some details implicating your husband and his infidelity, there is not enough information for the committee to pursue, not knowing the lady you were referring to, and whether this transfer went to her account. I am sorry, Philippa, you need to tell us who informed you and when?"

"I would never reveal that, James," she replied.

"In such a case, we will treat this discussion with you about Steve's infidelity as a domestic issue only. The Museum does not need to get involved. Still, you have not told me who asked you to contact me?"

"I will never reveal that, either."

"We will consider closing the meeting and dispersing after lunch. I would request you all talk about other issues, even the weather," said James.

The maid announced that the buffet lunch was ready and the menu included vegetarian and non-vegetarian items. Philippa, Steve and the chairman decided to miss the lunch and left. Barbara was impressed with James for making sure the museum committee was not involved in these family issues. Before leaving, Steve thanked James for confirming the source of the leak to his wife was unknown to most of the committee. Barbara wanted the chairman to attend a short meeting with her and James and he agreed to stay for lunch. After lunch, Barbara, James and the chairman went to the conference room.

"I have asked the other committee members to join us," said Barbara. "They should be here soon. I also requested Philippa and Steve to join us as well."

After a few minutes, all the remaining people had turned up.

"My inquiries," announced Barbara, "revealed that you, the chairman, disclosed the confidential information to Philippa, as you have known her since she was a child."

"It is a preposterous accusation, Barbara, please withdraw it," said the Chairman. "If you are proved wrong, then you should resign from the committee."

This annoyed the other committee members, who pointed the guilty finger at the chairman. The youngest member, working for the chairman's private company, said he was present when the chairman revealed to Steve's wife about the sexual relationship Steve had with Michelle. The member was threatened with the sack if he ever told others about this incident. So, the member decided to quit working for him.

"Unfortunately, the chairman has disclosed the details, and he vehemently denied it. He even threatened Barbara, that she should resign if proved wrong. So now he has been proved wrong, and are you, the chairman, leaving the committee?"

"I am tendering my resignation now," he said tersely and left the meeting.

"Philippa, my apologies for being so hard on you. We know the source, and we agree that your information was correct," said James.

"Where does Michelle live," she asked, "as I would like to meet her if allowed?"

"I will give you her address; she lives in a dilapidated flat in Hackney. I am not the one vetting people meeting her. You have to try your luck by visiting the flat."

He gave the details to Philippa. She took it and left.

"It was sad the chairman turned out to be the mole and had no integrity to admit his guilt," said Steve. "You are all better off without such a spineless chairman. His revelations have meant my divorce ASAP. I will pick up the pieces and not marry again, to save future divorces."

"It is decent of you, Steve, to admit your guilt," said James. "And I am surprised that following the present divorce, you are not thinking of not having future relationships with women except only not marrying."

"James," he replied. "I do not have strong principles like you. In my well-considered opinion, divorces have their prime cause in marriages. If there were no marriages, we would not have any divorces; fewer litigations arising due to divorces creating problems with the split of finances, property, etc. The world, in my opinion, would be a much happier place. Not many people can attract the opposite gender, and when one has such luck, one should make the most of it and enjoy it. Morality is want of opportunity. It is only for the purist like you, not the wider public. I am happy to be in the other sector to you. I want to take your advice when I mellow down later, but not now. I enjoyed meeting you all and hope to meet sometime in the future. Goodbye to you all." With that, he left the group.

"Isn't Steve a lucky fellow? Able to smile and plan even in times of adversity. Good luck to him," said Barbara sarcastically.

"We all agree with you, Barbara," said James. "Do you have anyone in mind as the chairman?"

"Two people want to join the committee, but both are below 45 years. The oldest member of the committee is John Spencer, who is with us, and he could act as chairman."

"I can act as the chairman after proper selection procedures in a day or two," said John.

Barbara asked the younger member who had resigned from the previous chairman's company about continuing in the committee. He agreed to continue. Barbara said she would ask one person from the waiting list to join. The meeting was over, and they all left for home. James returned home and updated Amma, Rose, his mum, Mary, Judy, Ethel and Michelle. Amma and others were pleased with the way the meeting had gone.

The following Saturday, Philippa came at 10 am as per Rose's invitation and was surprised to see James with several ladies, some she had already met. Rose introduced Mary, Judy, Philip, Paula, and Ethel.

"I am glad to see all of you living as a big joint family," she said. "I wish I had lived in a joint family. My dad was so wealthy he had little time for relations as he focussed on increasing his income and protecting it."

"We were a single-family unit initially," said Amma, "but due to Rose's marriage to James, things started to change for the better, and now we have a clan of seven families, and we meet frequently. Six weddings within the families have already taken place, and they all live close by."

"James, I went to Hackney with my maid but found no one living at the address you gave. One of the neighbors said that she came with a tall and good-looking gentleman and left with a case and bags a few days ago. I hope it was you as there are not many such attractive gentlemen around."

"Guilty as charged," replied James, "and as you made us go around in circles by not revealing your source, I played a silly game to waste your time. I am sorry, and do we have to discuss that now?"

"Not really," replied Philippa, "and I wanted to see her, admire her courage, and bring Steve to admit his misdemeanour to compensate adequately. I am not worried about money, but her involvement enabled me to divorce that bastard."

"If you were to meet her soon, would this sentiment change seeing her?"

"Not really."

James nodded to Rose, and she brought Michelle down to the lounge to meet Philippa. James asked Michelle to update Philippa. Michelle started from Amma asking her to stay here and all medical complications to the present day.

"I am pleased to see you but sad about the complications and miscarriage. Did Steve know about the miscarriage?" said Philippa.

"He came to see me after someone in the hospital told him about her losing the baby," said James, "and he had the audacity to ask for some repayment. I threw him out and shut the door saying good riddance."

"Typical of that bastard seeking money for drinks and womanizing!" said Philippa.

"We should only get on with 'here and now' topics," advised Amma.

The maid brought the twins, and strangely they went to Phillippa and held her hands. She hugged and kissed each one, holding their hands she walked with them. When she lifted them, the boy went for her breasts and she told all that they would have to watch this fellow not turning out like Steve! They were all amused by her comments. The maid and Rose took the twins upstairs for feeding.

"Philippa, you have not told us anything about your family," said James, "and we would like you to live near us, if I may boldly suggest. We are impressed with you as an elegant, sophisticated person who would enrich our group."

"Wonderful suggestion James," agreed Amma. "I am sure all group members would welcome her. We need to hear more about you, Philippa."

"As Amma said earlier, James, how you rope people in around you," she smiled. "My dad is a tycoon dealing in armaments, and the business is worth over five million. Due to our wealth, my mum heads several charities by holding honorary jobs. I have an older brother and sister, both married and living in Oz and the UK. My brother quarrelled with my dad as he did not study. He married, but his wife divorced him and got a settlement of £1 million, remarried, and lives in America. My brother was given half a million pounds and left for Rhodesia ten years ago. We have not heard from him since he left.

"Even after marriage, Rosemary's husband was a heavy drinker and womanizer. She divorced him and he left for South Africa with no settlement. Rosemary did not have any children. She works in my dad's company as a secretary in the UK, and she is good-looking but doesn't have enough skills to do the job well. I was educated to a Masters in Finance and made the error of marrying Steve, falling for his looks. My parents advised me to divorce him years ago, and I hesitated, which was a big mistake. He drained over half a million, and fortunately, the last affair with Michelle was a lifesaver for me in getting shot of him. I did pay him £30,000 as a parting gift, but he begged for more. My parents were happy to see him gone.

"I am very good at the arts and in freelance sketches. I started my Arts and Crafts company, and with my dad's contacts, I have a turnover of a million. We will not relocate to this area as we live ten miles away. I live separately in my own house, closer to my studio. I want all of you to come to my house next Sunday, for lunch, by 10 am, and stay till dinner."

"What an impressive family history, Philippa, said Amma. "Sad in some aspects but a relief in getting rid of daily irritants. Philippa, please try to consult James before you pick your next partner."

The twins came down and went to Philippa, and she played with them for an hour. Then, the maid announced a buffet lunch was ready, and they all joined by sharing two bottles of champagne. Philippa learned about the food requirements of James and Rose and agreed to send a car next Sunday for their Indian cook to help with the cooking.

"I'd like you to meet my cousins in the studio here, specializing in freelance portraits. I hope they can do business with you," said James.

"Funny that you've mentioned this at an appropriate time for my operation. The business is growing, and I need two specialists to take charge of my business. Let me meet and talk to them."

James took her to the studio and introduced Nicola and Vanessa. Philippa was amazed at their skills at such a young age. James left them to talk about art. He briefed others about how impressed Philippa was seeing their work and felt their future was secure. Amma felt his way of introducing people's skills had always resulted in getting the best results for everyone. Philippa and the two girls came to the lounge, and Philippa was excited that James got her the two very best artists for her business. She felt that the two introductions should benefit James to the tune of £50,000. But he smiled and refused to accept it. Amma told her about James's skills in stock trading and how many people want him to make their investments grow.

"I need to request James to invest £50,000 as my investment and I need to talk to you about it when you come next week," she said.

"We had better go to the other room and discuss it now," said James. "I want to spend the next week talking to your mum, dad, and sister and not spend the time on stock trading."

Philippa agreed and they went to the next room and spent nearly 40 minutes about BSL procedures and rules. She wanted to come during the week to open an account and transfer the money asap. James told her to deal with Rose for her investment. They all had lunch and Philippa left immediately with Nicola and Vanessa. Most of the others went to their rooms for siesta. Only Amma and Rose stayed in the lounge.

"Philippa wants to expand her business to £5 million with their help as she is making them partners with her," said James. "She wants them to stay with her from now on, and she took them to find out their response on seeing the facilities there. So, I think, just like Margaret and Clare, living in the museum, these two will live with Philippa from now on."

"James, I feel you allocate the studio for people with lesbian relationships. Am I right?" asked Amma.

"Nothing escapes your eagle eyes," he replied. "I told both of them all I knew about them. I cautioned Philippa about them, and she said she found out their tendencies. They would have an enjoyable relationship in her place from now on. Her parents do not know her sympathy for LGBT as they rarely meet due to their business commitments."

"Once they leave," said Rose, "we will only have relationships without LGBT scenarios in our group."

"It is true, but it is difficult to predict when people change.

We cannot take anything for granted for long," said James.

The following Sunday, the whole group, including all youngsters, their spouses, and children, went to Philippa's home for an extended stay beyond lunch. There they met her mum, dad, and sister. The introductions took nearly an hour. Her dad was keen to talk to James and they went to a separate room.

"Let me call you uncle from now," said James. "You have built a mega operation in armaments deals; did you have any threats from mafia groups?"

"It is funny you start with that; these groups threatened me several times in several countries, and I survived by bribing them. Once they received money, they protected me, which was most helpful. Initially, there was the threat of kidnapping my wife, Rosemary, Philippa, and others. But contacting the top man avoided any threat and ransom demands. I heard you are a successful trader, and would you be interested in my investing £100,000?"

"My returns are usually 1/4 to 1/2 % for each day, and you would double your money in your business a lot quicker," admitted James.

"Too true, but my business will disappear once I retire. My family are not interested, and I do not want them to be exposed to any threats or dangers. So, I have not told them that I sold my business for £4 million yesterday and from next month, I am a retired person. I will make the announcement later on. I am a small operator when it comes to the armaments business."

"I wish you a very happy retirement," smiled James. "If you relocate to our area, you can be in our group as the senior advisor, and we all would benefit. Until your relocation, you can join our lunch meetings every Sunday and other times."

"I would be delighted to join the group."

He wanted to hug James, but James asked for a shoulder hug only and briefly narrated the accident to his spinal column. Then, with tears, he gave a shoulder hug to James. They returned to the lounge and everyone wanted to know what they had been discussing. So, uncle told them about his retirement from next month as he had sold his business yesterday. James said their uncle would relocate to the area, and he would be the senior advisor for the group so that Amma could relax from next month. He and aunty would come to Sunday lunches and other meetings.

"I heard so much about you," said Rosemary. "And now I have lost my job, James please find a job for me asap?"

"James, I am so happy that you got the uncle to be the senior advisor to the group," said Amma. "It gives me more time to focus on the twins."

"James has the knack of getting the best out of people," said Philippa. "He got my dad to talk about the sale of the business, about relocating and becoming the senior advisor to the group. The more we move with James, the more we realize his strengths and skills. My dad, mum, Rosemary and I will come each Sunday for lunch."

"Please call me Alfred and my wife Alice from now on," said her dad. "James talked of the mafia threats, and then I mentioned the sale of the business, as the pressure was too much to handle. He is knowledgeable about my type of business. After lunch, I'd like to go home to sort out the sale details."

He and Alice left soon after lunch. Alice was impressed with the twins clinging to Philippa. She gave £20 to each of them;

Rose and James thanked her.

"I am speaking for Vanessa too," said Nicole, "that we would like to relocate to Philippa's house from next week. Thank you, Amma, Rose, James, and everyone for all the help you've given us so far."

"We were delighted to have you two living here," smiled Amma. "And hope both of your businesses pick up under the able guidance of Philippa."

"Speaking for Rose and me, I endorse what Amma has said," agreed James. "No doubt we will miss you but glad to know we will see you both on Sundays."

Philippa wanted to talk to James privately, and they went to the next room.

"James, you told me about the girls being in a lesbian relationship and how you were shielding them. I want to share some information with you in total confidence and hope you do not reveal it to others."

"I will treat your information in total confidence," he said.

"I feel the same way as the girls. I changed a few days before my wedding and made it clear to Steve about no relationship. It was good news for him to have his sexual affairs with others and demand money when he wanted. The divorce has liberated me, and I am so grateful to Michelle. My parents did not and need not know my inclination. I have had a few relationships before now, and no one suspected. Now it is perfect for us."

"I suspected for some time about you but did not want to say it.

Your secret is safe. You three can have variations of twosomes and even threesomes as you wish. Please make sure that the cleaning ladies do not suspect and gossip. I gave them that warning already. There are requirements to register with the same GP, but they do not flag up LGBT and staff in the surgery gossip."

"I never realized these details," said Philippa. "Please advise me. My few incidences were in a hotel or other houses, and I never thought of it. Would you please teach us how to keep the relationship secretive, like a brother to a sister?"

"Please come to see me on the pretext of your investment, and we can talk about the precautions from time to time. Never take pictures of you three without clothes or gadgets to stimulate your organs. Never tape your discussions in case you forget to put them away, and cleaners listen. The girls may work very late at night and get up after 11 am or later. The cleaners should tidy the bed in each of the three rooms each day after use. Ask your staff to change the beds after 2 pm, never in the mornings. Also, tell them that to save cleaning three bathrooms each day, you three would use any one of the bathrooms. They should clean the bathroom in the afternoons only. Being your own house, you can control these issues effectively. These precautions would save you a lot of heartaches later."

Philippa gave James kisses on his cheeks after a shoulder hug only. They both returned to the lounge, and Philippa mentioned that the girls were doing very well in their portraits. Amma felt that James would reveal it all later to them. They all returned home for a well-deserved siesta. James said there was nothing more to say as they talked about the girls' work. Now he had to find out what assignment to give to Rosemary asap. He asked her to come to the conference room for a short discussion.

He asked her what her skills were, what she wanted to do, and what her ambitions were?

"I am not skilled at all. Due to my dad, I worked as a secretary but was not good at my job. My husband wanted my money and started beating me while drunk. He visited prostitutes almost every night, and I refused to sleep with him. He became violent and started beating me. I had a guard outside my room to stop my husband from entering my room. I divorced him, and we did not pay him a penny. He emigrated to Oz and we haven't heard from him in six years. I would like to be independent and help others, who I don't know. I have no ambitions regarding my career, as I have enough money, and would like you to invest £100,000 for me. My dad is rich and we are the only two daughters to benefit. I might end up as a woman of leisure and help with looking after the twins."

"Rosemary, for the moment, I will let you enjoy all the leisure, and if anything crops up to merit your attention, we will review it," said James.

11
Between the devil and the deep blue sea

One Sunday, they met in Alfred's house for lunch, and the whole group met at 10 am for the morning coffee and a good natter before lunch, at noon. Then, finally, they all met in the lounge.

"We welcome Alfred and Alice to our group and future regular gatherings on Sundays," said Amma. "As they are new, I will ask everyone to introduce themselves and their family, and finally, they will talk about themselves. Please, Rose, you start first. It will take about an hour for our introductions."

When it was over, Alfred addressed the group,

"We are so impressed by how you all slowly grouped and started living together, and it is a sight to see. My parents passed away ten years ago, both due to natural causes. I was the only son. My dad joined his dad's business and expanded it to a quarter of a million, a high turnover in the early 30s. The armaments business is very shady. One had to bribe frequently to get contracts, which automatically generates enemies. We had three children, a son followed by Rosemary and Philippa. My son was a womanizer and a heavy drinker. He got married but ended in divorce. I gave him half a million as a one-off payment, and he left to go to Rhodesia. We have not heard from him in the last ten years. You have all met Rosemary and Philippa already. I sold the business because I felt Philippa need not deal with mafia groups. We are glad she is in the art and crafts business and doing well."

"My parents were teachers in a secondary school," said Alice. "My older brother and I were two children for them. Andy was a rebellious boy and ran away from the house before 18. We have never heard from him for over twenty years. He was good-looking and a womanizer. I had good features and I did A-Levels. During one summer, I worked as a receptionist, and then Alfred's company needed a receptionist. I joined his company as the salary was good and helped my family. Alfred fell in love with me, and we got married. Alfred has told you about my son and daughters. My parents passed away last year due to natural causes."

"Hearing the tragic stories of Ethel and Michelle and my daughter Rosemary," said Alfred, "I feel something has to be done to help protect women and girls from a similar predicament. I am not sure how and would welcome some suggestions."

"Alfred, it is a highly complicated and white elephant scenario. I am sure James will explain in detail," said Amma.

"For each woman falling into the love trap," said James, "one has to pay her salary, say £100 a month. Supporting them for six months means £600. For 1,000 such women, the money needed is £600,000. If one helps for a year due to pregnancy, it amounts to more than a million. All girls attending schools indulge in parties, drinks, dances, drugs, spiking of drinks, rapes, pregnancies, etc. One should be planning to help thousands of cases with the costs running into millions. It is better, Uncle, to stick to helping those cases that come our way. We should not think very big and drain hard-earned money."

"On reflection, I will stick with your advice and leave you to contact me if you need financial assistance to a deserving cause. I am delighted to be the senior advisor to the group," smiled Alfred.

Just then the maid announced that a family of four had come to see Philippa. She came out and did not recognize them and asked them to join the others in the living room and introduce themselves.

"I am the elder son of my mum and dad here," said the man. "It was strange that my youngest sister did not recognize me. I am Sydney, this is my wife Ava, and our two wonderful daughters, Amelia, seven years, and Mila, five years. I left ten years ago only due to my dad's pressures falling for the gossip about me. My mum begged me not to leave, but my dad had intense hatred, and he wanted me to get out of his life. I needed only £1,000 to go to Oz. My dad paid me £0.5 million, requesting that I never return to the UK. My sisters were too young to understand these things then.

"I will tell you all my side of the story. I was a good student and aimed to be a priest. My dad thought I was a rebel. I was a member of the local church choir. Two young girls in the choir enticed me to have sex with them on consecutive days. I misbehaved and it was consensual. The gossip started and we three left the choir. The tongues of the local community waggled to seedy proportions, naming me as a womanizer addicted to drinking and not good in studies. My dad swallowed all those despite my admittance of the sexual relations with the two girls, pleading and admitting we three were 17 years old. My dad told everyone I had gone to Rhodesia.

"The local Priest was happy that the three youngsters left the choir before the gossips started and saved the church from embarrassment. He also felt sorry for me as I was a good student intent on working in a church. He recommended me to the Priest in Melbourne for further training in the priesthood. My mum was helpless to argue with my dad and felt the two daughters needed bringing up properly.

"I left for Oz, went to Melbourne and reported to the local Priest. Even though he knew about my sexual relations, he felt that sleeping dogs should lie and no need to wake them up. I was keen on recording my guilt and underwent six months of severe penance and meditation to absolve myself. It impressed the Bishop and others in the hierarchy. I delivered sermons praised by the congregations, young and old, men and women.

"One family took an interest in me and invited me for frequent dinners.

The daughter was Ava, and she had a crush on me. I was 25 years old then, and her parents, with her consent, wanted a marriage with Ava. I wanted them to know my background before deciding. I told them about my past, including my toxic relations with my dad and my misdemeanours. I also told them to talk to the Priest as I needed his permission for my wedding. After a month, they decided to let bygones be bygones and move forward. I told them my dad gave £49,000 more than I asked for to come to Oz, and it is in a savings account earning 8% interest yearly.

"I told Ava not to make a mistake by marrying me and lowering her standard of living. My future was in working in a church helping the community. However, she was adamant about marrying me. Ava had an elder brother, married with two kids. He was looking after the family business of £6 million. Her dad gave Ava £2 million after the wedding. I have a modest income, and I live frugally in the church accommodation. She stayed in the church flat. We had Amelia after two years of marriage and Mila after two years.

"Rose," asked Amma, "please take Ava and the kids to meet Tara and the twins."

"Ava's mum and dad passed away due to old age," continued Sydney. "She felt that I should make peace with my parents and follow the religious principle of 'Forgive and Forget'. So, I decided to return to the UK. The local Bishop and the Priest in Melbourne arranged it with the Bishop for the Anglican church, where I was in the choir originally. I will be a minister for two years and then be a Priest. We came a week ago and found out the address details had not changed. My delight is in seeing Rosemary, Phillippa, and my mum. I hope my dad will forgive and accept the extra money he paid me with interest accrued until last month. Ava has not seen any of them, and I hope our family welcomes them fondly. "

"Sydney, your life in Melbourne has touched me more," said Alice. "I knew some lies your dad told to salvage his vanity in the misguided community. But I agreed with him all the time in case he lost his temper. I am happy you have come to our church as a minister, and I will see you every Sunday to hear the sermons. I hope Alfred also attends as an atonement for all the torture he put you through."

"Sydney, I sincerely apologize for the pressures I put you through," said Alfred. "I do not need the money. Please put it in a trust for Amelia and Mila. You and Ava have two lovely girls, and after all these years, you have blessed us with two granddaughters. I will attend church with Alice to hear your sermons, and please do tell in one of these sermons about a parent who had severely misbehaved and how he should atone for his sins."

"Dad, let us be happy that Sydney has come back with a

beautiful family," said Rosemary. "We should not think of separation as an atonement at this happy reunion. Let bygones be bygones, and let us move on as a united family from now on."

"James, you wanted me to be the senior to this group," said Alfred, "but with my behavior, I am not worthy. Despite age, Sydney is the right person to be the Senior."

"I understand you all meet on Sundays for lunch. I will be busy on Sundays," said Sydney.

"Alfred, you feel sorry for what you have done," said Amma, "and you have come to terms with your family. We are happy for you to be the senior for this group."

Philippa hugged Sydney and apologized for not recognizing him. She told how James had touched each of the adults and youngsters in the group. Sydney spent a long time chatting to James. After lunch, Sydney returned to the church, and Ava and the girls agreed to stay with Amma for a few days to get to know Tara and the twins. The local Bishop and the Priest were happy that Sydney had linked with his family amicably.

And what of the life of Steve Knight? He received £30,000 from Philippa as a parting gift, and he lived high, drinking and visiting brothels. He did not have a job in the museum and he needed women to satisfy his needs. However, he did manage to work for a small company. The secretary was over 50 years and was the wife of the MD of the company.

His brothel visits led to wrong contacts, and they were not in a professional class like him. But due to his drunken stupor, he rarely paid attention to it most of the time. On one of the days, while working late with the MD on an overseas visit, he tried his luck with the secretary, and she told her husband, who called Steve and fired him. So, Steve lost the regular income and reference to seek jobs with another company. He advertised as a freelance accountant for hotels, shops, and individuals. However, his income was low and not regular monthly payments. All this annoyed him, and mentally he developed a hatred for Philippa. He felt like the golden goose was no longer with him. He wanted to harm her. He also got annoyed with James for being a barrier to his getting a refund from Michelle.

Like fools and their money are soon parted, his money in the bank was less than £5,000. He started asking for small loans from his clients, and his credit cards were near their limits. He was no longer attractive to look at. With his breath reeking of alcohol, he lost most of his clients, and they took civil cases against him for their loans. He lost weight and frequented VD clinics to ensure he was free from disease. These affected his rational thinking, and his vendetta against both grew enormously. He wanted to hurt both of them but did not know when, where, and how. He expressed his evil thoughts to one of his mates from the drink and brothel circle. He did not realize that mate was an informer for the police. But the mate could not answer the queries of what, when, and how. The police thought it was bogus and ignored the comments of the informant.

Steve's debts were mounting and he frequently spent time in prison. His onetime professional career was in ruins. On one occasion, he gave Philippa's details as a contact. She told the police that she was his ex-wife and explained the circumstances, and he was relying on her as his cash cow. She showed them the court order for not contacting or visiting her. They gave a wide berth to all his claims from that time onwards. This treatment infuriated him, and he tried to bribe the guard to let him escape.

The guard told his superiors, and Steve's prison term got

extended by a few months. Steve felt trapped, and his anger boiled over on taking vengeance on both. He thought if James had not attended that committee meeting, he would not have resigned and his comfortable life would have continued. Steve was looking for solutions to where, when, and how. Then, he met Kevin, whose friend outside the prison was an expert in blowing safes, gained by working in mines.

Kevin said he could take care of Steve's problem but needed £1,000 paid upfront. Steve said he did not have any money here. Kevin's friend said Steve was the biggest fool. Being a qualified accountant, he could teach accounts to the prisoners, earn money, and get respected by the authorities. Steve thanked him for the valuable advice and contacted the prison authorities for teaching. They were pleased as it kept several prisoners out of mischief. Several weeks went by, and they were happy with Steve's role as a teacher. Due to the criticism from some inmates, who wanted him clean-shaven and not smell of beer, he started looking smart and reduced his intake of alcohol. He looked as he was while working in the museum. The prison authorities put Steve on a course to minimize his alcohol addiction. He was earning £200 per month.

There was a women's prison nearby, and the authorities wanted him to teach the women prisoners. He willingly accepted, and few of them felt a late evening coaching would suit them more. The prison authorities faced a dilemma. Was it prudent to send a seasoned womanizer to teach in a women's prison? The top man said it was economical to send him there. If he misbehaved, he should be charged £25 for each transgression.

"We will save money as he satisfies himself, and I am sure he would enjoy the sexual experience more than the money. We have a ready supply to meet his demands, and we do not have to spend our money from the government for this idiot."

They agreed with his logic. They told Steve the rate for each experience with women, and he did not mind the rate charged. Within a month, he owed more money to the authorities than they owed him for his teaching. Some prisoners had joined a short accountancy course, and they passed their exams with credit. There were about ten of them. The authorities promised to pay £100 for each successful candidate.

Steve appealed for early release, which was agreed. He wanted to teach the prisoners and the government paid him £50 per hour. He was a happy man with a limitless supply of women to satisfy him. Steve was allowed to use a small flat inside the prison complex, but no outsiders or prisoners were allowed to his flat. Despite these favorable changes, his vendetta never subsided. Kevin's friend, who was very skilled in opening safes, and a specialist in the use of dynamites, contacted Steve for the advance payment of £1,000 for fulfilling his vengeance.

In a moment of madness, Steve agreed to pay and stressed that there should not be any injury to the people, only to the property. Kevin's friend promised that he would stick to his deal to the letter. He wanted to know the information on, where, and when as he was an expert on how. The meeting would be in his ex-wife's house on Sunday at 10 am for lunch. The contact said that he did not have to go inside the premises to do his task. Steve wanted to pay half now and the balance after the job. Because someone might track bank credits and find him from the bank details, it was too risky for him, and his contact was interested in an upfront payment. Reluctantly Steve agreed to pay, but he would be in his flat inside the prison camp to have a cast-iron alibi. Steve gave the amount to Kevin's contact, and he stayed inside the prison camp.

Steve mentioned that his dad was a friend of Keith's who heard many nice things about James. Steve's dad did not know about Steve's womanizing in the museum but heard that he had been in prison, but did not know the reason, and his dad, 75 years, living on his own, since his wife died due to breast cancer, was in tears all the time. His dad also told Keith that Steve was crazy about punishing his ex-wife. Keith told him to ignore malicious gossip, but his dad was adamant it was true, as his contact worked for him before he started working for the prison authorities.

James was concerned that something bad was going to happen soon. So, he called Philippa and Alfred. All his family were there. He asked them to be quiet and listen to him patiently for a few minutes.

"I suspect that harming Philippa will happen soon, but I cannot reveal the cause. Let us plan courses of action. Philippa, please go with your mum, dad, and Rosemary on Sunday to the Anglican church to attend the sermon by Sydney. The girls will come to the old studio on Saturday and return to your place on Monday. Philippa, you arrange with a removals company to remove all your furniture and household items and store them in a safe place. All girls should meet at Amma's house by 9.30 am, but their cars, driven by a chauffeur to go to Philippa's house and leave. All families stay in their houses but send their cars, driven by the chauffeur arrive at Philippa's house, and leave by 9.45 am. All staff, kitchen, security, gardeners, etc., should leave the premises early morning and stay away for 24 hours. These precautions are to prevent any accidents on Sunday."

Alfred felt that James was panicking, but Amma advised him to listen to James without doubting him. All families agreed with Amma. Alfred then understood the similarity of a wavelength of all to Amma. They followed James's courses of action.

Around 10.30 am, there was an explosion and most of Philippa's house was damaged. The police and ambulance came to the scene, and to their shock, they found the body of a dead man in the rubble. The gardener had rushed to the house to pick up his garden fork and paid with his life. It became a criminal case.

Keith contacted Steve's dad and told him about the explosion and the death of the gardener. Keith also informed the police about what Steve's dad told him. Soon police found out about Kevin and his friend. They arrested him and filed a criminal case against Steve and his contact. With permission, Keith, James, Amma, and Philippa attended the court during the trial and saw Steve sentenced to 35 years of hard labor. Steve did not show any remorse and thus ended the sad episode of vengeance-laden Steve. No one felt sorry for him, including his dad. Sydney was amazed at the foresight of James perceiving the danger and saving others, including his family.

Philippa saw another bigger house near Amma's house and bought it with the help of Nicole and Vanessa. The insurance company would not pay for damages due to the explosion, but they did compensate the gardener's wife. Alfred apologized to James for his hasty remarks.

"Amma," asked James, "do you think many evil eyes saw the clan living together? Do we have to stop meeting frequently? How do we protect ourselves in the future?"

"We have to analyze the situation," she replied. "There is still one person we have to track and find out in all our families. So, I leave you, James, to clear this person from our concern."

"Thanks, Amma for putting the ball back in my court. I will find out the whereabouts of Rosemary's first husband in the next six months. We will continue with our present arrangement of meeting every Sunday. We set a time limit for a response about him in six months. If not, we forget about him. We now have 15 seniors in the group, and all are going through the exercise regime."

"I agree with you, James," said Rosemary. "Let us move on and live happily hereafter."

"Amma, no matter what happens," said Rose, "we should continue to enjoy and never curtail our group activities."

Five months passed. The twins started going to the kindergarten class, and all the girls went to the same school where the mothers in the group sent their children. There was no news from the private investigator about the whereabouts of Rosemary's ex-husband. The regular meetings took place on Sundays. Sydney was busy with weddings on Saturdays and the group rarely met Sydney for lunch. The group did start attending Sunday mass in the morning from 10 am for an hour and only then meet for lunch.

Another two months passed. Then James had a call from the private investigator:

"I have some bad news for you. The ex-husband of Rosemary did not travel to South Africa but Rhodesia. He was there with his parents for four years. It appears they met with an automobile accident four months ago and did not have any papers to identify them for months. All three were DOA at the hospital. I was the first one to enquire about them. The authorities contacted me, and with the photo given to me, they traced. Unfortunately, it seems there was no forwarding address in the UK."

James thanked him and informed all the others. Then, in muted silence, they heard the sad news, except Sydney, who prayed for the souls of the three people.

James, Alfred, Amma and Rose agreed to meet regularly on Sundays and other occasions and felt they should enjoy the children during their formative years. Alfred with Amma decreed that they should listen to James as he was the guiding light to all the adults and children in the group.

12
Epilogue

The group spent their lives happily helping each other and the children did well at school. However, years rolled by and the young children turned into teenagers giving pleasure but also putting families under a lot of pressure due to changing demands of their peers and new expectations of the times. All the changes provide the subject matter for an exciting sequel to follow soon.

———

Available worldwide from
Amazon and all good bookstores

———————————

www.mtp.agency

www.facebook.com/mtp.agency

@mtp_agency

Michael Terence
Publishing

www.ingramcontent.com/pod-product-compliance
Lightning Source LLC
Chambersburg PA
CBHW022209050726
47590CB00002B/720